Save the Last Stall for Me

A Collection of Writings by Members of

Suburban Write People:

Gail Cohen, Jennifer Djordjevic, William D. Hicks, Barbara Moriarty, Jim Szczepaniak and Barbara K. Yohnka

PublishAmerica
Baltimore

ISBN: 1-60836-980-3
PUBLISHED BY PUBLISHAMERICA, LLLP
www.publishamerica.com
Baltimore

Printed in the United States of America

Table of Contents

Section Four: Sink or Swim

Section Five: The Outhouse Chronicles

Section Six: When Love Leads to Hot Water

Section One: What Mom Never Told You About Public Restrooms

From the Desk of Mr. Man-ners

Dear Mr. Man-ners:

I've got the perfect question for you, because it's a manners question. Recently, I was at a party and was waiting in line for the ONE bathroom in the house to become available. I waited and waited and the line of people got longer and longer. Then I started hearing all these weird noises coming from inside. This went on for a good 20 minutes. I knocked and asked if everything was okay. I didn't get any response. Ten minutes later (a good 30 minute wait) two people came out of the bathroom tucking in their shirts. I believe the other person must have left the line and crawled through the window because they had to go that bad. How rude is that?

Stuck Waiting

Dear Stuck Waiting:

I bet they told you to wait in line for a brain too—and you're still waiting! Don't you know what was going on in there? Sex. S-E-X. No one "snuck in the window"—the two people were in there all that time. Together. This type of behavior should not be tolerated. How rude to do this to the host! Whatever happened to "private" moments? Other people's bathrooms are not one's personal sex stall! Get a room. Get a car. And if you're even thinking of doing this in MY house—at my party—get the hell out and have your sex after you leave! Be aware that I know how to open my bathroom door without a key—so think twice before you partake in this kind of activity at my place: I will expose you and your partner's business and your sordid "small" mindedness and small everything else so my partygoers have a good laugh. Plus, I will expose the naked ass truth about you on the Internet. Remember this, because no one will ever get stuck waiting to use the bathroom at my party—at least not because of some sex-nanigans or Tom-fool-arounders!

Mr. Man-ners

Up Against the Wall

by Jim Szczepaniak

We were visiting New York City and got together with a couple who had just moved there. Belinda, whom my wife used to work with, thought it would be fun to have afternoon drinks in one of the trendy new boutique hotels that were all the rage at that time, the early 1990s. The place was owned by the guy who opened Studio 54 and designed by French hot-stuff designer Phillipe Starck. I was out of my element in a hotel of hipness.

We had been walking around the city on this harshly hot and humid day and, underestimating the distance to our meeting place, had to run the last few blocks to make it on time. By the time we got there, my wife and I were soaked with sweat. Eyeing the chicly dressed young people who were entering the hotel in front of us, I feared we were a bit under-dressed.

As we were "greeted" by the lounge hostess, tall and willowy and clad all in black, I was not even sure they would let us in.

"Hi, we're just coming in for a drink," I said. She eyed

our Midwestern tourist garb, sighed deeply and led us, not saying a word, to a dark booth in the back corner of the black-and-black room.

"We're meeting some friends," I said, wanting to let the hostess know so when Belinda and John came in she could bring them over.

"How nice," she said, almost under her breath.

A few minutes later Belinda and John had joined us, and we were looking at the drink menus. That's when I learned that a beverage in this place costs more than I usually pay for an entrée at home.

"Isn't this fun?" Belinda giggled as she put down the drink list. "I think I'll have a chocotini!"

"What's wrong?" my wife asked me. "You seem grumpier than usual."

"I just have to go to the bathroom real bad," I said, "I'll be right back."

Down the hall were two doors next to one another, each marked with some kind of hieroglyphic symbol. How were you supposed to know which was which? I waited a minute to see if someone would come out, giving me a hint. I felt a pain below my stomach as I realized how close I was to having an accident. Still no one was coming out.

Just then, I saw a twig-thin woman, all in black, coming down the hall with a clipboard in her hand. She looked like she worked here.

"Excuse me, can you tell me which one is the men's room?"

She stopped abruptly, made a loud tsking sound and rolled her eyes.

"Well, the door on the right, of course," she said, shaking her head.

I ran to the door and pushed it open. It was dark in here too. Faint canister lights in the ceiling bounced some illumination off stainless steel walls and stainless steel sinks.

I walked past the sinks to where I expected urinals to be. Nothing. Just the steel wall.

That's okay, I thought. I'll use a stall.

There were two of them, each with a door climbing almost all the way up to the ceiling. Both doors were closed. Someone was making a lot of noise in one of them and from the sound of it, he was having a hard time of it. I knocked on the other stall door.

"Can't you see it's occupied?" a man yelled out. "Wait your turn!"

God, I wish I could. This was nuts. There must be another room with the urinals. I looked up and down the length and width of the space. Nope, this is it.

My mind raced through options: I could wait for a stall to free up. I could use the sink. What else could I do? Go back out and ask a hotel employee where the urinals were?

All right, I guess it's the sink. My God, what if I get caught?

Just then, a sleek young man dressed all in black

walked in. He casually strolled right up to the stainless steel wall and unzipped his pants. I stared without meaning to. Just as he started to urinate, a gentle waterfall cascaded down the steel from the ceiling.

I ran to the wall. My stream rushed into the waterfall. My sense of relief was matched only by my disbelief that I was in fact pissing on the wall. I looked down and saw that a narrow trough carried the water away to a drain on the floor.

"Pretty cool, huh?" the guy next to me said. "It runs on a motion sensor."

As I walked back to our table, I was beginning to think this place was not so bad.

"How was the bathroom decorated?" my wife asked.

"You have to see it to believe it," I said. "I don't know what the women's room is like," I said. "But I'm guessing it's not as much fun as the men's!"

At Your Service

by Jim Szczepaniak

A mortifying experience: I walk into the bathroom of a restaurant or club and see a restroom attendant—or, as I call it, a toilet slave. This person greets me with something like, "How are you doing tonight, sir?"

I want to reply, "I was doing fine until I walked into the bathroom and saw you, but now you are making me feel uncomfortable and guilty." But I do not say this because I realize this is a human being who has probably taken this gig only because he has to make a living somehow and could not find a different job.

Yet I wonder what the hell the management of this place is thinking. If this were a bathroom in a big sports stadium and they had an attendant who was mopping up piss pools around the tank urinals and replacing quickly depleted toilet paper and cleaning up vomit from the young yokels who come to the game to get drunk and stupid, that would be great. But of course, those places never have bathroom attendants.

But here, in the overpriced steakhouse, you have the

black man—and I'm sorry, but it's always a black man—who will hand you a paper towel after you wash your hands, as if it is too much trouble for you to pull your own towel down from the dispenser. In a slightly more "upscale" joint, he will interject himself between you and the faucet to squirt a burst of soap into your hands as you begin to wash. In a really swank place, he will have men's cologne to offer you, as well as mouthwash and—yes, since this is supposed to be a great place to bring dates—condoms.

Am I the massuh on this plantation or what? What kind of person would actually feel pampered by this treatment?

In theory, after I've encountered a toilet slave, I tell myself that next time I will hunt down the manager of the establishment, protest the practice and vow that I will not return to this place of business until they have freed the slaves.

And yet, despite my abject aversion to the bathroom attendant, I laugh each time I recall one of the most memorable public bathroom experiences I've had.

It was back in the days when disco was king. Qiana was the queen of fabrics and people got their groove on by doing the Hustle. Since I was only a kid and new to the nightclub scene, I had no problem getting in since this was an all-ages establishment.

I was agog at the environment, swept up by the swelling dance music and the flashing lights and fog machines and reflections off the rotating mirror ball. While Alicia Bridges was reminding me how much I love the nightlife, I had to boogie off to the bathroom.

Awaiting their turns at the urinals was a virtual line dance of Tony Manero wanna-be's. The hair, the gold chains, the tight pants, the platform shoes—what a sight! I envied the guys their disco ballsiness, knowing that I could not aspire to that style.

What drove that sentiment home was the man standing in front of the mirror when I went to wash my hands. He was availing himself of every type of service the bathroom attendant was handing out. First, he took a lint brush to the guy's rust-colored polyester suit. Then, from behind, brushed him with practiced efficiency from shoulders to hips.

"You're looking good, Sir," the toilet slave said in a lilting accent that sounded like it came from the islands.

Our disco king, a swarthy fellow, pulled his dark black hair back at both temples and smoothed it behind his ears. "Hairbrush?"

"You got it, Sir," the attendant said, handing him a styling implement.

The king ran the brush through his abundant hair. "Spray?"

"You got it, Sir," the attendant said, spritzing a cloud of chemicals that quickly drifted across the room.

"Cologne?"

"Yes, sir. What is your pleasure, Sir?"

"Brut®? You got Brut?"

"Indeed, we have Brut, Sir! The company says it is the essence of man!" The attendant picked up the bottle from his collection on the sink and handed it to the man, who slapped the liquid liberally behind his ears and on his neck.

"Now this," the disco legend said, spreading open the collar of his disco shirt. "What do we do about this?"

"What do you mean, Sir?"

"It's looking a bit clumpy," the man said, gazing at his curly tufts of chest hair in the mirror.

"Oh, we can take care of that, Sir."

The attendant walked over to the corner of the bathroom counter. There was a jar of disinfectant filled with blue liquid. He pulled a black comb from its watery depths. "Would you like me to comb it for you, Sir?"

"No thanks, I can handle it."

The king undid the last two buttons of his shirt and dragged the comb through his chest fur—once, twice, three times.

"Thank you," he said, returning the comb. I could see several curly hangers-on clinging to the comb, even from where I stood.

The attendant calmly picked out the hairs and deposited them into the trash bin before dropping the comb back into the disinfectant.

I forgot to pay attention to whether the disco king tipped the man. But he should have.

That's what I call service.

Tales from the Head

by Jim Szczepaniak

Walking into any bathroom that's not your own is always an adventure because you're never quite sure what awaits you. Walking into a strange bathroom makes me realize why "There's no place like home" is such an oft-cited cliché. My bathroom might not be the best, or the cleanest, but it's mine.

Despite the kvetching that is about to follow, I will admit upfront that dealing with strange bathrooms does make me appreciate the fact that I'm a man. In most cases all I have to do involves standing in the right place, unzipping my pants, tapping my kidneys, zipping back up, washing my hands and leaving. Unlike women, I do not have to worry about certain things every time I enter a bathroom, such as the "do I sit or do I squat?" dilemma, remembering to check ahead at each visit to make sure there's toilet paper, or adding another five or ten minutes to wait in line before I even get into the john, as seems to be a given at any big public event.

Still, problems lurk. Scary things await the unsuspecting visitor.

(Not so) automatic flush toilets. What a great idea to put automatic sensing devices on toilets so you don't have to choose between several bad options: 1) touching the germ-covered handle; 2) using your foot to flush the thing (and, if you're in a place like a ballpark where the floor is always wet, maybe having a very unfunny slip-on-the-banana-peel moment, putting life or limb at risk); or 3) leaving your bathroom handicraft for the next person to appreciate.

So sensors are a great idea. Too bad they almost never work.

When the thing doesn't flush, I check out the toilet to see if the rocket scientists who designed this particular model gave it some kind of emergency flushing mechanism, a button, perhaps, or a hidden lever. Unfortunately, I did not get a degree from engineering school and can't figure it out. So I wave my hands frantically to and fro in front of the sensor like some semaphore signalman on speed. Nothing. Now it's a challenge I must win. I sway from side to side a few times, figuring that maybe the sensor wants to see larger body movements before it will flush. Still nothing. I turn around and sit down on the toilet, then stand up. After all, this is how the sensor is supposed to work, right? I am now doing full reps of toilet sit-ups, stand-ups, and squats, 10 times each. Still, no flush.

Oh, well, I tried. I leave the stall defeated. The toilet won this time.

The flip side, of course, is the automatic flush that just won't quit. You walk into the stall, the toilet flushes. You step toward the toilet, it flushes again. Start to unbuckle your belt: flush! And so it goes. As a man, when I have to sit, the last thing I want is an unexpected stream of water dripping and swirling around my more vulnerable parts, so the overeager flush is one of the nastier bathroom bummers.

The "fancy" guest bathroom, or "Look, but don't touch." This particular scenario usually takes place in the homes of older aunts and people whose living room couches are protected with plastic slipcovers.

Aunt Clara's guest bathroom: As you enter, you will notice it is meticulously kept and almost spotless, except for the barely perceptible specks of dust on the plastic flower arrangement that stands in a light blue glass vase at the corner of the sink counter. The vase has several seashells pictured on it. The bathroom's theme is seashells. The shower curtain features beige and white seashells on a blue background.

Four tiny soap seashells, two blue and two white, sit in a scallop-shaped soap dish. Two pink starfish soaps sit alongside; Aunt Clara prides herself on her decorating skills and doesn't mind making a daring design choice by mixing things up.

After you do your business, you go to wash your hands

and realize the soaps have never been used. And no wonder: getting them wet might compromise the delicate shape of the seashells. But there is no other soap to be seen.

Well, you didn't get your hands dirty. So you just rinse them off under the faucet, then go to wipe your hands.

The larger towels on the main towel bar have a blue background and white lace trim along the middle and bottom, with embroidered silk seashells. The towels are hung carefully so that the lace trim is aligned just so between the two towels, creating a perfect symmetry that may not be disturbed. Except for the price tag that dangles down from the one on the right.

Hands still dripping, you turn back to the towel bar that hangs over the toilet. Two sets of towels nestle alongside each other, each group consisting of a dainty fingertip towel at the top, a middle-sized one behind it and, behind them both, a longer bath towel. The size of the last resembles something you might actually use to dry your hands, but again the lace and satin embroidery make you hesitate.

Just as you think, "What the heck, I'll just wipe lightly," you notice a small note safety-pinned to the closest fingertip towel. In perfectly controlled cursive, it reads: "For special occasions." You're not sure if this visit qualifies, so you wipe your wet hands on your jeans before leaving the seashore.

The cushy tushy bathroom. This variation is meant to make the user more comfortable but ends up having just the opposite effect. It features a bathmat set made of plush shag carpeting, preferably in jungle green or bruise purple. The set includes the bathmat itself, a matching shag toilet tank cover and a horseshoe-shaped foot mat that snuggles up against the base of the toilet. The toilet tank cover is perfect if you're afraid of having your glass of water leave a nasty ring on your sink countertop. The floor mat is perfectly placed so that anything that misses the toilet will conveniently drip or fall onto the shag rather than messing the floor.

Adding to all this cushy bathroom comfort is the padded toilet seat. This squishy wonder will give your rump a rest while you relax on the toilet. It also makes an obnoxious noise, like a whoopee cushion, when you sit on it. Just make sure you don't rustle around too much on the seat, since the slippery vinyl covering is not so easy to clean, especially after it gets a tear or two and the stuffing tries to escape.

The scary guest bathroom. You are staying overnight at a relative's house or a friend's house, not because you really wanted to. Maybe the hotel was too far away. Maybe your hosts said they would be mortified if you did not take advantage of their hospitality.

You kind of had your doubts. You've been to this house and know it's not being used as a model lab for the local health department.

Now, coming on to bedtime, your hostess says she has just "freshened up the guest bathroom and put out some towels. Have a nice relaxing bath if you'd like," she says. "We'll see you in the morning."

It's too late in the evening to make alternate arrangements. You go into the guest bathroom. Your worst misgivings are confirmed.

As you enter, the smell of pine-scented bathroom deodorant overwhelms. It is working hard to mask the underlying odor that is reminiscent of old socks, sour milk and dirty diapers.

You turn on the light; the bulb on the left side of the sink flickers and burns out; the bulb on the right reveals a cracked bar of soap on the counter that looks like it has not been used in quite some time. You turn on the water, thinking you'll moisten the bar and bring it back to life. You try to pick up the bar, but it sticks to the sink. You pry it off to find several dark curly hairs nestled underneath.

No big deal, you tell yourself. All you need to do is take a leak, take out your contacts and brush your teeth.

When you raise the toilet seat, you see yellow and brown spots on the underside. Should have taken out your contacts first. No problem. You've got your lens case and cleaning solution. You turn the water back on and try to lather up the soap. No suds. You rub the sad bar between your hands. Nothing. This must be soap, right?

You figure the friction alone has made your hands safe, so you take out your contacts, looking in the mirror, but not too hard, because it's got blots and spots of stuff on it. You suspect the last guests flossed their teeth in front of the mirror and it hasn't been cleaned since.

Brushing your teeth is the only thing left, but you forgot your toothbrush. And toothpaste. You figure you'll just use your index finger and borrow your host's toothpaste. You open the medicine cabinet and find the crinkled tube of paste.

How bad can it be? You take it out. Not much paste left. Just a squeeze and you'll be fine. You unscrew the cap. And there it is: a dark, wiry hair.

Okay, no need to brush. Just go to bed. Check out the shower in the morning, but know you don't have to take a shower. Tell yourself you'll be back home tomorrow night, in your own bathroom.

Close your eyes, take a deep breath and repeat those words from your childhood: There's no place like home, there's no place like home...

Privy to Private Conversations

by Tracy Ruppman, Guest Contributor

Who hasn't been jarred out of a dramatic scene in a movie theater by a Nelly ring tone? Or been annoyed by the person next to them on the bus recounting their debauchery the night before? Who among you hasn't been cut off by an inconsiderate driver more focused on their conversation than the 3,000-pound vehicle they are propelling at 40 mph?

Nearly everyone has a cell phone and they are used everywhere and anywhere, making private phone calls a thing of the past. People talk on cell phones on the street, in the library, waiting in lines, in meetings, on elevators, but of all the places I've had to tolerate, it never ceases to amaze me how many women like to talk on their cells while using a public washroom. Do they think the stalls are sound proof? And I began to wonder, does this happen in the men's room? I offer you a sampling of cell phone conversations I have overheard while using public bathrooms.

Mind over matter over toilet: While dining in a suburban Chicago restaurant, I excused myself to use the restroom. In the stall next to me tan, perfectly pedicured feet said, "Mom. Mom! Listen to me. You have to take your medication... Mom, the doctor said you have to take it... Well, It's going to take some time to get used to. You may feel funny for a couple of weeks... If the Zoloft doesn't work, we can ask him to change it to Prozac, or something else. But you have to take it, Mom. You have to give it a try before we can change it... Mom, stop crying... Would you take the pill, please! Mom, I have to go. Daniel is waiting at the table. Take your pill, go to sleep and we'll talk tomorrow... Goodbye, Mom." She sighed as she hung up the phone, and I stayed in my stall until she left. To avoid the discomfort...to avoid the uncomfortable silence...

Cheaper than getting a babysitter: As I stumbled into the bathroom of a North Side bar one Saturday night, I overheard an African-American woman with strappy, high-heeled gold sandals apparently scolding one of her children, "I don't care who started it. I said, I don't care. Put your brother on the phone. Boy, I'ma whoop your ass when I get home if ya'll don't stop. I don't care. Don't make me come home early! Now, get to bed!"

Pancakes or toast / sausage or bacon; did you save room for dessert? After eggs Benedict in a favorite Sunday brunch spot on the North Side, I went to the bathroom to freshen up. I discovered a twenty-something woman, sitting on the counter, talking on her cell: "Yeah, he's hot...We went to eat at that Cuban place on Ashland and then salsa dancing... Yeah, he knows how to move—on the dance floor and in bed! Yes, I did! Girl, he was good! We're having breakfast right now... It's true what they say about Latin men. Good God, it was the best sex I ever had!"

Your wait time is 45 minutes: While visiting the bathroom at a major university in downtown Chicago, I overheard a frustrated 40-something woman declare, "I'm not near my computer right now... Can you just tell me...will I see that link when I get back to my computer? No, I told you, I'm not near my computer right now." FLUSH! "Can you just tell me what I will see? No, I can't write it down right now. Just tell me...I'll remember."

Secret agent man: In a downtown, late-night restaurant, I followed a tall blonde woman wearing three-inch spiked heels and a black miniskirt into the restroom. She placed a call and entered the stall next to me. "Sergei? I know, I'm sorry... If all went well, Jeanne and Jane are with Luigi... No, I haven't heard from them...I think that's good. They would've called if they hadn't found him... Yes, I'm sure... You don't trust him?...It'll be fine. Jeanne and Jane can handle it... Call me if you hear anything."

Oh, no you di-ent! In another Chicago bar, I overheard this Jerry Springer episode in the making: "Don't even lie. I saw you looking at Tamara at Jameka's party last week. You want to get with her? You're a lying sack of shit! Your boy Marcus already told me what you said about her, Asshole! Last night...No, I didn't fuck him! Please. Keshia says his dick's smaller than yours...That's right, I know you fucked her. That bitch'd fuck anybody... I'm done talking to you...No, I'm done with you...Okay...Call me later."

Calling Dr. Phil: In an office building in Oakbrook: "I don't blame you for being upset. He's an idiot and an asshole... You can do better than him... Yes, you can, Rhonda...He's not good enough for you and he's not worth your tears...If he loved you he would have treated you better... Like not calling when he's gonna be out late, like not coming home at all...and spending all your money on blow... Jeez, Rhonda, how much does it take? I would have left that asshole a long time ago... I know you're not me, but you gotta stand up for yourself...Rhonda, he's not worth your time...I've gotta go. My boss is on my ass today. I'll call you after work."

And now a word From our sponsor, Kleenex® tissues: Between classes at another Chicago-area university a young woman wearing bright pink flip-flops and pale pink nail polish on her toes entered the stall next to mine, crying uncontrollably. She paused and took shallow, stuttering breaths before answering. "I...I...I don't under...stand... Why? But..." She gasped for breath. "You said...you loved me... Can't we talk about it? But...why?" She cried harder. "But I can do that... Yes, I can... I'll try to...Hello? Hello?" She wailed louder. I got out of there as fast as I could.

What Do Women Do in Restrooms?

by William D. Hicks

I'll admit it. I'm a guy. A man. A typical male. Well, maybe not typical. Anyhow, I've often wondered what women do in the bathroom besides the obvious. So, I asked a friend. Okay, so I've known her since college and she's more like a sister.

"What is it women do in the washroom that takes so damned long?" I asked.

My friend —name changed so every woman can think she's the one—said, "Oh, did I take a long time?"

I thought about it for about a nanosecond and said, "No. You were as fast as a man. But what takes most women..."

She gave me the sign, the one that means girl hygiene issues. Okay, I lied there is no such sign—but there ought to be one—men hate the words!

"They can't all be doing that," I said.

"Well," she admitted, "You're probably right. I don't really stay in there long enough to know."

The subject was dropped. But not for long. My mind

considered all the things women could possibly be doing, while their men waited, pacing, as if expecting the second coming of Christ. The world was created in seven days after all—figuratively, because we all know it was millions of years—and that's how long it takes for a women to return from the restroom.

Anyhow, here are my thoughts about what women do in restrooms.

Bikini Waxing—okay, so most of the women in there couldn't possibly get away with wearing a bikini, but that doesn't mean they don't enjoy the smooth feel after waxing!

Showering from the sink—well, I guess that's more like a sponge bath. Are they practicing for when they have to bathe their newborns? Or does this particular women's room have their favorite soap, the one they can't find in the store? Or the one they can't afford in the store?

Shaving, before the bikini wax—Or would the bikini wax make this unnecessary? And why do women complain about stubble so much when they all swoon over Antonio Banderass's five o'clock shadow?

Brushing their teeth—being sure to floss, probably with the strings on that bikini plus the wax.

Writing a grocery list—well, they do have to sit down; they might as well make it worthwhile. But I'd hate to see what that list looks like afterward. Bet they never forget toilet paper if they do this while relieving themselves. Perhaps this is why they do this in the restroom; the feel of the toilet seat is like having a string tied around their ass!

Writing a novel—given the amount of time they spend in the bathroom, it's not surprising that some of the longest books in history were composed while a woman was on the toilet! by a woman, and by a man waiting for that woman! Think Tolstoy.

Applying nail polish—is the women's room a covert nail salon or what? Okay, I could say the obvious, like how men could paint a 12-bedroom house inside and out while a woman is in the toilet—using it, supposedly. But let's just say that if it takes them this long to polish a few nails and do their duty, well, most men wish these women would polish their knob that well!

Having a conversation on the cell phone—let's just say a woman once told me that the tinkling I was hearing was running water and I didn't believe it for a second. Running water does not make plopping sounds!

Finishing paperwork from the office—again, I'd hate to see the stains on that paperwork, let alone handle it. They should just use it when they run out of TP—since most women complain about this anyhow! You never hear a man talk about this issue—because men can rough it! They have the snail trails to prove it.

Or, perhaps women do some other thing in the toilet—do they shampoo-lather—rinse—repeat? Or are they answering emails/surfing the Net/listing and selling on eBay/trying on dresses/knitting sweaters/cleaning the bathroom from top to bottom with an old toothbrush they carry just for that purpose?

Whatever it is women do for so long, men are just dying to know and they will speculate about what it is until the end of time, which by any reasonable standards is usually when a women comes bounding out of the restroom, laughing and giggling with her "new-found" friends, as if she is part of some secret society!

A Deep and Probing Inquiry into

Men's Restroom Behaviors

by William D. Hicks

Society has a myriad of books on socially acceptable behavior, including How to Tell Dirty Jokes During a Religious Sermon; Eating Broccoli: How Not to Get It Between Your Teeth and Being PC: How Correct Is It To Steal the Abbreviation of Something Else? All these rules are for a "polite society."

Yet no one has published a "bathroom" book. No, not one of those "readers" for men and women who feel the throne is their personal library or bookstore. I'm talking about a book covering socially acceptable public men's room behavior. If such a book existed, it would answer some of the following unanswerable questions:

The Gas Chamber:

I think anything having to do with passing gas (or blaming the dog for breaking wind) brings a laugh to my typical male beer belly.

Is it okay for a man to fart loudly in a restroom? If not,

where? Standing at a urinal or only in the solitude and seclusion of a stall? Does he have to apologize in here, too? And if he can't fart here—where can he fart? And if he farts in a forest and no one is around to hear...is it still funny?

Hands-on Handyman:

Why do men put their hands/arms on the wall when urinating? Are they too tired or too lazy to support themselves? Or are their bladders so excessively full, the weight excruciating, that they are forced to lean against the wall for support? Are they showing off or being lazy? And after touching the wall, or the urinal plumbing, how can they continue to do their business and shake the dribbles off? Isn't this wall germ ridden? Do men worry about these things, or is this strictly the realm of women?

Toilet Territory:

Why is it that when there is a toilet seat with a split front it's always wet? Bad aim? Good aim? Or are these men just marking their territory?

Garbage Can Games:

Why do men insist upon over-filling one trashcan in the men's room, even when there's a half-empty one available? Are they too lazy to walk the extra half-foot? Or too afraid to test their shooting skills, because with their truly bad aim they will surely miss—just as they missed the urinal?

Doing Business That's Not Bathroom Business:

Why do some important meetings take place in the men's room over the urinal walls? And why do these men tend to stand at two opposite urinals—leaving one between them—forcing newcomers to listen to a conversation not intended for them? Urinating is not a team-building activity. Get a room—a meeting room.

The only possible appropriate talking in a men's room should be "Hello" or the unutterable nod. Do not ask me, "How ya doin?" or I might respond, "I'm doing my duty." Do not ask me, "What's up?" or I might respond, "Are you trying to proposition me?" Do not ask me, "What's new?" or I might respond, "The brown spot on my penis. I hope it's just a freckle."

Is it ever appropriate to shake hands in a public restroom after urinating? Even after you have washed your hands? Scientists claim urine is one of the most sterile liquids in the human body. But God knows how sterile it is once it gets out. Yet, men blow their noses—then shake hands—but would likely refuse to shake someone's hand after they just urinated. Does this make any sense?

Male Modesty:

What is it with men and being pee-shy? Those walls between urinals were supposed to alleviate this irrational fear. And it is unreasonable, because what's the worst that can happen? Is another guy really going to out urinate you, then point at you as he's leaving and laugh uncontrollably about your unsteady stream? Because you both know he sounded like a geyser while you sounded like a leaky faucet.

Why do some men stand at the urinal when it's obvious nothing is coming out? Are they waiting for "Divine urination" or a fart that will release their "imprisoned" urine? Get over it—other people are waiting. You lost the battle. Now, let those of us who sound like Old Faithful use the urinal.

One Size Doesn't Fit All:

Why is one urinal installed that is five feet lower than the others? Is it for children or vertically challenged people?

Unhygienic Hygiene:

Why do men insist upon brushing their teeth in the one and only sink that is stopped up? There have to be seven million more germs in a public men's room than in their bathroom at home. Do they have a doctor's appointment, date or job interview?

Why do men leave toilet paper, a germ barrier, on the toilet seat after they're done? Is it so they don't have to touch the seat? But didn't they already touch it to put the toilet paper down? Are they afraid of their own germs?

If the toilet paper runs out in your stall, is it permissible to run, with your pants down, to an adjacent stall, because you don't want to mess your underwear? Or would you have to run with your pants up, thus assuredly messing your underwear, into the women's room next door? Or would it be better to use paper towels, or the revolving cloth hand towel, instead?

Does the five-second rule apply to food or drink that

hits a men's room floor? Don't even ask me why I want to know.

Calling for a Cleanup in Stall Two:

Why do men insist upon making/taking cell phone calls in the restroom—even if they are not themselves using the facility? Surely the call-receiver hears everything, including all that flushing. "No, I did not have any dairy. Yes, I know how it doesn't agree with my digestive system. Honey, I promise you that's not me you're hearing."

Condom Nation:

Why are condoms sold in men's rooms? Condom machines should be in women's rooms—after all, they're the ones who make men wear them.

The Few, The Proud, The TP Reserve:

How many men does it take to change a roll of toilet paper? Too many, obviously, because even when there's TP in reserve, there's never any in the holder. You thought this was going to be a joke.

Potty Room Poetry Analyzed:

Who is Lee? And why does he like pee? And why would he want to set his penis free, while he's on one knee? And why are so many men's restroom walls cluttered with so much rhymed reading material? Who thought up this crap?

American Idol of the Potty:

If one knows they're going to make obnoxious sounds in the stall, should they flush madly to mask the noise or would it be better to hum the "1812 Overture" loudly to accompany the cannon blasts?

I may not find any of the answers to these questions in my lifetime. Still, someone needed to pose the big questions. Plus, the little ones.

Section Two: Wrenching Tales from the Loo

From the Desk of Mr. Man-ners

Dear Mr. Man-ners:

They say you're supposed to sing "Happy Birthday" when you wash your hands so you know that you've spent the right amount of time lathering up. I'm wondering if you could suggest some other tunes. People keep rushing out and buying me useless gifts because they think I'm hinting around. Don't you think it's about time it dawned on them that I don't have a birthday five days a week?

Soap Opera

Dear SO:

First off, I do hope you wash your hands the other two days of the week. Next, I say SO what! I've never heard of singing songs when you wash your hands. Maybe whistling while you work—but wishing while you wash—I think not! Still, I can suggest some songs—Try You're So Vain by Carly Simon. With the lyrics "I bet you think this song is about you, don't you, don't you," you should reduce the amount of gifts you get, as well as the amount of friends you have. Or maybe sing The Bitch is Back by

Elton John. With the lyrics "I can bitch, I can bitch, 'cause I'm better than you, it's the way that I move, the things that I do" your friends won't be buying you birthday gifts, they'll be buying you Midol® for your PMS. Or if you're on a college campus try singing Disarm by the Smashing Pumpkins. With the lyrics "The killer in me is the killer in you," instead of getting birthday gifts you'll be getting a free overnight stay at the local jail. I'm going to end my response to you with Go Away Little Girl by Donny Osmond. With the lyrics "Go away little girl. So go away little girl. Call it a day little girl" it totally sums up my feelings about your trivial question. For God's sake woman, there are people who can't even get into the bathroom, let alone wash their hands. See my previous letter.

Mr. Man-ners

The Djordjevic Compromise
by Jennifer Djordjevic

"Eric," I huffed at eight o'clock on a Saturday morning. "Get up! We're not gonna let another weekend get by without doing something about the bathroom."

Of course, I could have let this weekend slide just like all the others, but I had a deadline to meet. My dad and his wife would be arriving in two weeks and there was no way the four of us would survive using a single bathroom.

Plus, the last time they were out for a visit we talked about grand plans to finish the upstairs bathroom before they came back. "You'll love it," I'd said. "We're actually going to get started on it this week." That was two years ago. I looked at Eric and smiled. We had good intentions. "Now that we're rested up, we can finally get something done."

"Come on!" I nudged him again. He was doing a great job of pretending to be asleep. Eric's left eye opened. "Dad will be here in two weeks."

Those seven magic words did the trick. "Okay, let's get going," Eric muttered groggily as he swung his legs over the side of our bed. Twenty minutes later we were in the truck headed toward the first home remodeling store we encountered.

I was excited about finally starting the project. My hopes were high that we'd have a good time in the process. But then I remembered what it was like when we did the rest of the house years earlier.

"Grab a cart," Eric ordered. Task completed, I fell in line beside him and tried to look half interested as we perused the aisles of tiny electrical and plumbing parts.

"Did you bring the list?" List? Oh my God—it was the strangest sense of déjà vu I'd ever had.

"What list?" I said with an emphasis on "what." "We never had a list because you said you'd remember what we needed." My first deep breath of the day came and went.

"Forget the list—let's just grab what I know I can do right now." Eric guided the cart down the plumbing aisle first. "We'll need a p-trap for the bathtub. Hey can you grab that ½-3/4 copper reducer?" He pointed in the direction of the item. I'm sure I looked like a deer caught in the headlights of a semi-truck.

"We'll need flux and—crap—do you remember if I picked up any EMT conduit at home?"

I was beginning to lose hope of understanding anything when Eric asked, "What kind of toilet do you want?"

Hallelujah! A word I could relate to.

"What do you think?" I asked. After all, he was much more familiar with toilets than I.

"I just don't want something that's too small. You know, where the opening is too small?"

No, I guess I didn't understand. Granted, styles ranged, but a toilet was a toilet right?

"Eric, just pick something out. Two weeks. Remember?" Jeez, if I could only use those words whenever I need to get something done. He pushed the cart around with purpose and $400 later, we left awash with hope.

As we headed toward home, I realized I was not looking forward to the task ahead—taking a 300-pound cabinet fitted with a granite countertop up the stairs, across the landing and into the bathroom.

"I don't know how the heck we're going to get that sink up the stairs," I hinted, half-hoping he would say he'd ask the neighbor to help. No such luck.

"We'll get it up there between the two of us. It's not that heavy."

When we arrived back home I immediately went to the kitchen sink and began washing dirty dishes. I swept the floor, tossed in a load of laundry, rearranged the refrigerator and wiped down the shelves. I cleaned out the junk drawer and organized bills—anything to keep myself busy before Eric insisted on carrying the monstrous beast of a cabinet up the stairs.

"Jen, you ready to help?" Eric had a look of pure determination on his face.

I eyed the vanity. "Eric, that thing is really heavy—why

don't you ask one of our neighbors to help?" It was as if I'd slapped him in the face.

"Are you kidding? We can do this ourselves. Actually, I could probably carry it up alone if I had to. I'm not asking the neighbor." Another testosterone-driven challenge had arrived. Eric began to pull the cabinet, which was resting on a piece of cardboard, to the stairway.

Good plan, I thought. Let's not ask the neighbor for fear of bruising our pride. Men!

"Fine, but I think it would be best if I went first and helped you to guide it up the stairs." With both of us in position we began the laborious task of maneuvering the cabinet. I tried my best but, as usual, I just wasn't up to the task.

"What are you doing up there?" Eric asked, his chest heaving, clearly strained by the effort of supporting the majority of the weight.

"What do you mean, what am I doing up here—I'm helping—that's what I'm doing."

"Well your help is not working! Jeez, I can't support this thing by myself." Eric's face was a bright red portrait of determination and strain.

In hindsight, I now realize that my next choice of words weren't the best.

"Maybe you should have asked the neighbor to help like I said."

If Eric could have hoisted that cabinet on one finger and thrown it at my head he probably would have. "That's it! Get out of the way!"

I barely escaped before he gripped the sides of the cabinet and miraculously, through some source of strength only angry handymen and husbands exhibit, shoved the cabinet the rest of the way up the stairs.

Eric's face was purple.

"Do you want some water?" I asked lamely. "You look tired."

*   *   *

A few days later we were ready to start the finishing work. "Hey, let's get over to Home Depot tonight and get the rest of the stuff we need. We can pick up Frankie's on the way home," I suggested as a peace offering. I hate the place, but knew that Eric would jump at the possibility of downing a jumbo hot dog with the works.

I'd been thinking for months about the bathroom's color scheme and overall look. Beige and cream with black accents. Classic elegance.

"What kind of tile do you want, Jen?" Eric walked the length of the aisle where the boxes were located. He turned around and held up a plain, beige square. "I was thinking this one," he said.

"Okay, enough joking," I said, handing Eric a ceramic square that I'd chosen. "I want this tile." I'd looked at them in the past and thought they'd complement the bathroom perfectly.

"Oh, come on!" Eric whined. "That's not going to look good up there. I've been doing bathroom remodeling for years and I can tell you right now it's going to be terrible."

"It will look good and it's what we're going with." I stood my ground and he shrugged, loading up the tile on the cart before heading for the next section. "I'm picking out the faucets and shower head," Eric informed me confidently. "I know exactly what I want."

"How could you know exactly what you want since you didn't even ask me first?" I complained, hoping he'd fall for my plan. "It's my bathroom so I should pick." I was being a complete princess about the whole thing and enjoying every minute.

"Here we go—perfect!" Eric beamed as he lifted a showerhead the diameter of a full size Frisbee. He held it up and away from himself as if admiring a brand new baby. I felt dizzy. There was no way I could live with that fixture.

"No-no," I insisted. "I'm not Andre the Giant. I don't need a shower head that's bigger than I am." I grabbed the box out of Eric's hands and put it back on the shelf. As fast as I put that box down he grabbed another one.

"Voila!—this is the one we need!" Eric answered, presenting his other choice with a flourish. He held up a three-head system with two hoses and 10 massage options.

"Okay—enough! I get your point." He'd only wanted to be a part of the process. "But we have to agree upon all the stuff we're getting," I said knowing that compromise would be torture for both of us.

To my amazement, we spent just under two hours

choosing everything we needed to complete the project. On the way out to the car I thought about how lucky I was to have married Eric, the perfect handyman.

As promised, we stopped and ate at Frankie's before going home.

"I think we did a good job together," Eric mumbled, his mouth full of jumbo hot dog.

"Yep—we did pretty good," I said trying to picture how the Frisbee faucet would look in the shower. "I really think those tiles are going to look fabulous."

Within a few days the entire bathroom was done. And it did look wonderful.

"You know," I said, holding Eric by the waist, "this really did turn out to be a beautiful room, didn't it?" We gazed into the bathroom and admired our work.

"I agree—I didn't think those other tiles would have looked great but you were totally right about these."

"And," I conceded "I didn't think that showerhead would have worked in here, but it does. I'm really impressed, Mr. Djordjevic."

With only two days to go before my dad arrived, I busied myself by hanging the shower curtain, fluffing the towels, filling the soap dispenser—all the details needed to create a welcoming atmosphere. When my dad and his wife arrived we got them settled and then proudly showed them the new bathroom.

"We just finished it a couple days ago," I winked at Eric. "We promised, remember?"

Eric did the honor of showing them the faucets and demonstrated how everything worked. "We've got our hot and cold water here," he said with a grin, flicking the sink faucet on and off. "The shower head is almost like a waterfall; it's so big."

For the final flourish, Eric flushed the toilet. "A working toilet!" he exclaimed.

Just then, steam started to rise from the bowl.

"What the...?" Eric muttered as he looked into the bowl to watch the piping hot water gently fill the bowl. In the chaos of finishing the bathroom the pipe connections must have been inadvertently switched, so that hot water filled the toilet whenever it was flushed.

At this point, there was nothing to do but laugh.

Who knew Eric was so talented he could produce a bathroom with a toilet that doubled as a self-cleaning commode?

An Easy Fix

by Barbara Yohnka

When I first began watching Home and Garden Television, every program intrigued me, but I found myself spending far too much time watching the shows. Every time a new feature was added I felt compelled to watch it at least once. To catch all the shows I wanted to view I had two video recorders and a DVR, thinking that might solve my taping problems, but watching the programs proved just as overwhelming. I was using up sick days to catch up on my viewing and losing sleep too.

I tried to catnap on my planning periods but my colleagues complained about my snoring in the teachers' lounge. Consequently, I began watching shows that dealt with organization because my home had become almost uninhabitable due to my lack of interest in housekeeping. My kitchen overflowed with delivery boxes because I didn't have time to cook, unread newspapers piled up on my counters, and essays I had brought home to grade taunted me, seemingly pleading for red ink as they spilled over the sides of several book bags that lined my foyer.

Washing clothes became a problem, too. I tried to do laundry during commercials but being able to fast forward through them left me little time to perform that duty. I got to the point that I wore a different colored sweat suit every day just so I wouldn't have the dilemma of choosing what to wear and thereby eliminating ironing as well.

When my sister suggested that I might have a problem, I knew I had to do something.

I could continue down the treacherous, obsessive path of watching all HGTV programs, or I could choose one topic or one room in the house upon which to fix my attention. After careful consideration, I chose to view shows that only dealt with bathrooms. They were usually the smallest rooms in the house, and with a coat of paint and a few accessories, could appear totally transformed, providing me with the quick fix I needed to satisfy my decorating urges.

In addition, I cancelled all my home magazines except those that focused on restroom remodeling. With a few, simple, handy tips under my belt, I was ready to try out my new skills. I would no longer be merely an observer of beautified bathrooms but would now be the person responsible for producing pretty powder rooms.

A few days later, I got my first job, a spare bathroom in the apartment of a friend who worked out of her home as a psychologist. She wanted to spruce up the space by changing the wall color, the window coverings, and adding new lights and fixtures.

Armed with primer, paint brushes, rollers, duct tape, electrical tape, a staple gun, scrapers, a drop cloth and the latest copy of Decorating a Bathroom on a Budget Using Feng Shui, I began my first renovation.

I did fairly well removing the flocked wallpaper and the remnants of the inch-thick paste that remained. I began applying primer and was working at a pretty good clip until I had to paint around the window. Remembering one of the prep techniques featured on Save my Hideous Bath and being a perfectionist, I scraped the sill to remove all the loose paint. That's when I unearthed a colony of bugs about the size of a small third world country. I got rid of them by using the duct tape and dangling them off the back porch as a lure for the neighborhood rat. I felt bad for them but, after all, I had a job to do.

Next, I prepared to paint the ceiling. Since buying a ladder wasn't within my budget for this first job, I positioned myself with one foot on the folding chair my friend had provided and the other foot on the toilet's lid. I was craning to reach the corner of the wall near the top of the window when the chair began to slide. I thought the toilet tank would stop the skid but I miscalculated. As my foot slid off the commode, my other leg cramped and I tried to grip the edge of the chair with my toes.

A couple of hours later, after Steffeny returned from an emergency intervention, she found me on the floor mumbling something about a trapeze, which actually might've been a nice addition to my equipment.

Fortunately, after my own trip to the emergency room, and learning I was concussion-free, I returned home, promising Stef to make good on my vow to finish her bathroom.

About a week later, the walls in the bathroom were painted a sprightly celery green, the fixtures had been changed to a brushed silver, and a simple, bamboo Roman shade covered the glossy, white enameled window. There were only minor problems installing the new light sconces, but after I turned off the power, I finished the job shock free. In regard to the faucet, since Stef had already hired a plumber to do some work in the other bathroom, his timely tips assisted me in completing that job. Because cleaning up was part of my duties, wiping up the water from my initial plumbing accident actually helped me accomplish two tasks at once.

The only promise I couldn't keep was tiling the floor; however, since it was to be featured in next month's installment of Decorating on a Budget... Stef agreed the tiling could wait until I'd gone through the "course work." My payment for this job? A free counseling session, on my remodeling addictions, if I ever needed it.

My next job came when I went to visit a friend in Las Vegas for the Christmas holidays. Ellen was planning to retire at the end of the school year and had purchased a house as far away from Chicago as possible. She invited me to stay with her, and then drive back to Chicago. I was eager for any opportunity to escape a frigid Chicago winter. While I was there, she suggested, maybe I could give her some helpful hints on how to freshen up her master bathroom. That sealed the deal!

On one rare overcast desert day, El and I made a list of things we needed to get from the home improvement store to update her bath. The wallpaper needed to be removed, the wall "eruptions" had to be repaired, and towel bars and a mirror were to be replaced. As if that wasn't enough, she wanted crown molding and new baseboards installed, plus new faceplates on the outlets, new knobs on the vanity and a litany of minor fixes we probably wouldn't have time to do. We bought scrapers, primer, paint, brushes and rollers, spackle, a hammer, drill, screws, nails, and a level.

Returning home, we laid out our materials and headed for the master bath. The first step was tearing off the wallpaper, so I used a water-filled spray bottle to speed up the process, and loosen the glue remnants. While the wall dried, El and I began to remove the towel bars. One side of the bar came off easily; however, the other screw seemed embedded in the wall. Upon further inspection, we learned that the screw itself was somehow tethered to a stud in the adjacent bedroom closet.

"So what do we do now?"

"Not to worry. We've already pulled the screw out as far as it will go. We need the hammer to pull it out the rest of the way," I said, trying to sound authoritative.

El was eager to show her prowess with the hammer, the

only tool with which she'd had any experience. She firmly gripped the screw between the hammer's claws and pulled with all her might. Nothing happened. She thought that I should try, but I had the arm strength of a two-year-old so I vetoed that suggestion. I told her to try again and I would put my arms around her waist while she attempted to yank out the incorrigible screw.

"Ready?"

"Okay."

We both pulled with all of our strength. I fell backwards into the shower, throwing the door off the track and Ellen finally got the screw out but left the hammer's claws inside the wall.

"Oh my God! My wall's ruined!" she exclaimed. She apparently hadn't noticed me struggling to get up out of the shower stall. Once she did, she yelled, "And my shower door's broken too!"

"No, the door's not broken; just off the track," I said, leaning on my elbows. She finally lent a hand to help me out of the shower. I put the door back on the track easily.

"What are we going to do now?"

"Chill. This is an easy fix," I said. That was my answer to every jam I'd ever been in and it was never easy. Because I didn't want to alarm her, as hysterical as she was, I spoke to her calmly, like a dog, and told her we'd go back to the home store, buy some joint compound and mesh and patch it up good as new. I'd seen it done on TV but had never actually done it myself but it made as much sense as anything I could come up with on my own.

I suggested that El take a break and I'd begin priming the walls. I stirred the primer, poured it into the pan, and began painting. Then a strange thing happened. While I was rolling over the supposedly clean area, the paint started to bubble. This couldn't be good, I thought. I tried the paintbrush. Same effect. I rolled on some more primer and the bubbling continued. I decided to finish rolling the entire wall, let it dry, then check back on the bubbling. It was a good time for lunch anyway.

"Are you finished priming?" El asked.

"Just the big wall. What would you like for lunch?" I asked, pulling out deli meat and bread from the refrigerator.

About 45 minutes later, El had calmed down. We'd had lunch and were ready to continue work on the bathroom.

When I entered the room, the entire primed wall had bubbled. El, about six inches taller than I, saw it the same time I did.

"Why are there bubbles on the wall?"

"That's a good question but I'm sure there's an easy fix."

"Where have I heard that before?"

"Let me figure this out before you have another meltdown," I said. El stomped out of the room and went outside to have a cigarette.

I'd read the directions on the primer. I'd read the part in the magazine and on-line about how to remove wallpaper. The method I'd used had been used before. There was only one thing to do.

"El, I've got a solution," I stated. "We have to texturize the walls."

Ellen just rolled her eyes, grabbed her keys, and her checkbook and we headed for the home store. While I inventoried the texturizing products, I sent her to find a shade or blinds or some window covering for the bathroom window so she wouldn't bug me while I was trying to figure out which product was best for the job. Eventually I found one that was like sand that one added to paint to texturize the walls. The paint would be thicker, and we would need a different roller, and probably another gallon of paint, but it would take care of the bubbling problem.

The next item on the agenda was the joint compound and mesh. That really was an easy fix. I just had to convince El.

Armed with our supplies, we went home and prepared to complete the job. The first thing I had to do was fix the gaping hole in the bathroom wall. Ellen couldn't even look at it without getting hysterical. The directions were simple, really, and after applying the mesh and smoothing out the edges with the joint compound, the hole was patched. El was dubious that it wouldn't show after we'd painted but I assured her the hole would be indistinguishable from the rest of the wall's surface.

After seeing the patch job blend in with the rest of the wall, and feeling more confident that things were looking up, El joined me in applying the sandy texturizing paint on the wall. The roller was considerably heavier but eventually all the walls were covered. There were a few areas where the "peaks" had to be knocked down a little to prevent scratching an arm as you walked by, but overall, the job was finished.

We slept in the next day but then after breakfast, checked the paint, the patch, and pronouncing them good to go, began to install the new towel bars. Fortunately, at Ellen's height of six foot two, installing the bars a little higher, above the patched area, look as if they were made for the spot.

My second bathroom redo was complete. My friend was happy with the results despite the few bouts of hysteria. However, I was exhausted! Remodeling bathrooms was hard work. As a result, I decided to switch from HGTV over to the Food Network. How hard could it be to become a gourmet cook?

The Desperate Person's Guide to

Bathroom Cleaning

by Gail Cohen

Disgusting! That's how I describe the least desirable, but most frequently used, room in the house. When it comes to tackling the job of cleaning my bathrooms, let's just say that doing the job sober isn't one of my strengths. Do you wonder why? Dirty tubs look like oil slicks, sinks are gunk-covered—and toilets? We won't even go there.

Avoiding the job altogether would be possible—just not in this lifetime. Fact is, crawly microorganisms regularly form large trade unions, making Machiavellian plans to morph into uber-germs capable of taking us out on a whim. It's a no-win situation if we expect to keep our families healthy and our guests from having to be transported to the nearest ER after using the powder room.

Desperate for a solution—and certain you share my aversion for this thankless task—I kicked my right brain into gear and came up with a short list of ways all of us can have a spotless bathroom without lifting a finger. Since many of these ideas are one-time-only fixes, you may need to try all ten to get the job done regularly. One thing is for sure: You won't find more creative ideas in any other cleaning guide on the planet.

10. Use your pet to clean the can. C'mon. You've spent a fortune on your pet, forking over half your salary for food, toys and vet visits. Whiskers and Bowzer say thank you by regularly offering disdain and a smelly butt, then hog your bed by sleeping horizontally so you're left clinging to a small sliver of the mattress. To add insult to injury, they show their love by leaving a coating of hair all over your pricey, upholstered furniture. There's more. They drive friends away by hounding ultra-allergic visitors and show their utter disregard for your clothing and heirlooms by romping over them at will. Such examples of pet payback make my case for why you should enlist yours to tackle the world's most hated job.

Now, I'll share the methodology. Encase your dog or cat (snakes work too, but don't try this with hamsters as they squeal really, really loud) in a tailor-made Swiffer® suit (see sidebar), and then lock her in the bathroom while using a fan to blow the smell of their favorite food under the door. They'll run wild and capture grit, grime and dust as they struggle to get free. The terrific benefit of this method is that it can be used whenever you like. It's not like the dog or cat is going to strike or leave home! Come to think of it, you can save a helpless creature destined for euthanasia by adopting a few to do the job. Hell, you could rent out the critters.

9. Train a toddler to clean the loo. As most parents know, kids are eager to please when they're young and since they're born tabula rasa (Latin for "we had no idea cleaning a bathroom is considered by adults to be a disgusting job"), they'll never know they aren't required to do this nasty work. As a matter of fact, we believe that indoctrinating kids while they're young will program them with an irrational need to clean bathrooms. By the time they need therapy to deal with their bathroom hygiene obsessions, you'll no longer be footing their bills! Here's the drill. As soon as your child, a sibling's child or even a neighbor's child is old enough to take direction (no need to explain why you're borrowing a child; parents are always in need of a break), dress him or her in a custom-made Swiffer suit (you know where to look).

Feed the child as many sugar-filled cookies as they can keep down, put on some Hannah Montana music and turn them loose in your bathroom. They'll crawl, prance, roll, boogie, slither and do what little ones do when they're high on sugar and left to their own devices. Be prepared for anything when the child comes down from the sugar rush and you've got most of the job done without lifting a finger. Repeat as needed or double the cleaning time by putting kids and pets into the room together. Oh, and it's never too early to start scouting the neighborhood for replacements when the child begins to age out and expects to be paid.

8. Call in the Health Department to sanitize your bathrooms. If you've let your bathroom go for an inordinate amount of time, drastic measures will be called for. An anonymous call to the Health Department, if worded properly, may be the answer you seek for a proper cleaning. Before you make the call, however, you must find a nice collection of bugs ready for release. When the folks in hazmat suits arrive, set the parasites free and feign amnesia. "Who am I and how did I get here?" is a good start. Authorities will haul you off to a mental health facility and clean your abode to prevent an infestation of Biblical proportions throughout the neighborhood. This technique is particularly effective if you live in attached housing because condos and townhouses are prime targets for opportunistic, fast-spreading pandemics. Warning: this solution can only be used once.

7. Hire a high school student addicted to speed to zip through your rest rooms. For minimum wage and a handful of drugs, your bathroom can look brand new in just a matter of minutes. Since your recruit will likely bring their own IPod®, there's no need to provide music or a Swiffer suit to get the job done. If your teen is high enough during the cleaning process, there's a good chance that he or she may finish up your bathroom, whip through your kitchen, then move on to the rest of your home, as well. Given the upside of this cleaning method and the abundance of kids on drugs, you may want to put this particular method at the top of your list—especially if

you have a teen in your home who has been doing a piss-poor job of hitting the books despite being up and alert for days on end. There's a bonus here. Some kids are so caught up in the frenzy, they race out the door without requesting their salary.

6. Feign illness to enlist the help of others to clean your bathrooms. Even in today's narcissistic society, there are people who live to serve others and can be counted on to appear at your side when health issues arise. Once your loo reaches a state of disgust that literally makes you sick, research popular illnesses on the Internet, choosing one that most closely matches your ability to act out the symptoms. Don't go for the terminal stuff as shaving your head and playing the chemo patient won't fly with many of your close cohorts—especially if the disease's onset appears shortly after you've begun an aggressive aerobics program. When you figure out which illness works best for you, take to your bed, start making phone calls and it won't be long before friends, relatives and neighbors appear on your doorstep with cleaning buckets, tea, casseroles and offers of help. Since this method of bathroom sanitation can be employed only once in the city in which you reside, I recommend moving often to get the most bang for your illness buck.

5. Post your obituary and friends and relatives will clean up for you. It's a fact. Dead people don't clean bathrooms. If getting your shower sanitized has become a matter of national urgency, you may have to resort to a

solution more radical than #6. The Obituary Plan is just such a tactic. Posting your own obituary doesn't take much effort, but you must have all of your dead ducks in a row before you contact newspapers because once the notice appears, you'll be required to disappear, pronto. You may wish to call relatives before you disappear, dropping hints about how you have included a token of your love in the will. Allude to the fact that they will get their legacy during a pre-planned party at your home.

Call Peapod® to fill the refrigerator with enough beer and wine for an army (food will be taken care of by mourners), then head for a spa or undisclosed destination worthy of Dick Cheney. You'll need time to figure out the story about how you came back to life (resurrection has already been taken), but even if nobody's talking to you when you return, your bathroom will be fit for the wake of your dreams.

4. Put your home on the market and let the realtor tackle the cleaning. Your realtor will tell you that one of the first things you need to do to attract buyers is to clean up and weed out, but if you are simply too lazy to do that, my solution is to market your house as a fixer-upper. Let the whole place go, even if the neighbors picket you for turning the subdivision into a blight-ridden area that plummets real estate values like the stock market crash of '29. Use this method correctly and you won't have to move the first time you try it! Convince your realtor that you're too busy to clean. If you've found a broker desperate

enough to do what it takes to close a deal, you're golden. Once your place goes on the market, the realtor will hold an open house. Station yourself nearby (wear a hoodie, even in summer) and warn all browsers that the place is riddled with termites. If these winged wood-eaters are not native to your area, substitute a local bug. When every visitor takes a pass on the home, tell the realtor you've decided to take the place off the market. Deflect blame by telling him or her that you've seen many ineffectual realtors in your day but they were the worst. If you live in a city with a phone book full of real estate firms, you might have discovered the way to get perpetually clean bathrooms ('til one savvy broker gets wise and visits a local gun show).

3. Recruit an out-of-work senior as a permanent bathroom cleaner. Today's job market for post-50 workers is a bitch these days. Locate these folks, contact their spouses, and then offer to relieve them of the burden of having a perpetually out-of-work mate for whom health care, food and maintenance have become burdensome. Once you've negotiated the best deal, staff up and assign tasks. If your senior is desperately trying to hold off on filing for Social Security benefits because they're not vested until they turn 80, use cash under the table as a bargaining chip. Alternately, if your senior is already on Social Security, more cash will buy you a happy camper. To spruce up your offer, up the ante by throwing in a subscription to the AARP magazine and all of the

Depends, Viagra, Polygrip and acid reflux meds your senior desires. Time off for visits to the proctologist, heart specialist and arthritis clinic will be so appreciated, you might be able to offer less than the minimum wage, thereby putting a dent in McDonald's recruitment numbers!

2. Attempt suicide and get multiple offers to sanitize your bathrooms. If you watch crime shows, you know that suicide attempts may prompt forensic specialists to appear on scene and once they're done making sure the attempt is self-inflicted, companies formed specifically for post-evidence clean up are called to the site. Your suicide attempt will get you out of the house while all the work is done. By the time you return from the hospital and/or your short stay at a local mental health facility, your lavatories will be pristine. I can't emphasize enough how important your choice of suicide methodology is; you must replicate the real thing, but never maim, cripple or injury your body. Such actions are unsightly and leave one vulnerable to feigned suicide lawsuits brought on behalf of county or state government. I recommend choosing from methods other bathroom-cleaning-averse folks have tried:

- Drink a small dose of carpet cleaning solution.
- Indulge in a snifter of antifreeze.
- Munch E-coli or other germ-laced leftovers (see sidebar).
- Choose any of the agents described in the book I Felt

Like Such a Loser, I Even Failed in my Attempt to Kill Myself, available from KevorkianBooks.com.

Do not—I repeat, do not—try any suicide method involving self-mutilation! Having a clean bathroom should never put your body at risk for ugly, permanent scars.

1. Torch your bathroom if you need a truly radical solution. Nobody brings more water to a party than the fire department, so all you need to get that loo spic and span is a match, shower curtain and phone. When the bathroom gets to the point where ordinary cleaning methods simply will not do, light the shower curtain, dial 911 and scurry to your front yard so you can bravely wave in the first hook and ladder rolling into your cul-de-sac. I recommend avoiding this method if you prefer see-through plastic shower curtains. The odor of decomposing plastic can be toxic and will creep into drywall and remain with you in much the same way curry can result in a kitchen that smells of a trip to Bangladesh long after you've returned home and unpacked. As a precautionary note, don't be tempted to replicate my friend Brenda's action when she tried this years ago! Waiting in the yard for the fire trucks with a pan of brownies and a banquet-size pot of coffee may seem like a welcoming touch (it did to her), but those guys are smart and will see right through your desperation for an industrial-strength bathroom hose-down. Motives apparent, your water-bearing saviors may turn away, leaving you to witness your home's destruction. But, come to think of it, having

no bathroom means your problem is solved.

How to make a Swiffer suit

1) Measure the wearer.

2) Purchase enough Swiffer cloths to cover the body.

3) Use your sewing machine to create a sturdy garment that won't rip or fall apart.

4) Add Velcro snaps or a zipper to make it easy to put on and take off.

5) Need multiple Swiffer suits? Purchase raw material from a warehouse club.

How to grow your own e-coli

1) Don't clean the bathroom for months.

2) Use toilet scrapings to start a culture in a Petri dish (Tupperware® will not work).

True Confessions: Beauty Secrets of a Middle-Aged Man

by William D. Hicks

I'm no Adonis. But like all men, I enjoy looking my best. However, it's gotten to the point where I buy so many beauty products I can deduct them as a business loss on my taxes. A loss, because they're obviously not working. As if things couldn't be worse, after using all these beauty aids I smell like a cross between Hawaiian suntan lotion, a doctor's office and a Grand Canyon mule. Such is my vanity.

My morning bathroom ritual entails taking a shower using a beauty bar that has yet to make me beautiful, plus a shower gellee scented to "cause" a state of euphoria. If I could only get my $50 back for the 1-oz gellee—I'd be euphoric—I promise. Used together, they gently cleanse, without damaging my skin.

Next I apply a mint herbal shampoo to my hair. It's made without animal testing: Who knew animals liked to taste-test shampoo? I lather, rinse and repeat. Then I apply an equally strong, but differently scented, coconut and pineapple hair conditioner. My hair smells like a mint julep and a pina colada accidentally mixed together. "You got your mint julep in my pina colada!" "You got your pina colada in my mint julep!" Two great smells that don't smell great together. Afterward, I towel off. Not too hard, as I don't want to damage my sensitive skin.

With my towel now wrapped firmly around my growing (too many shower-inspired mint juleps and pina coladas) waist, I apply a gel shaving cream. It glides onto my face—then foams—I look like a rabid dog! It has aloe in it. It has vera in it. Knowing that I shouldn't shave too soon after showering because I have a sensitive beard and my follicles must soften up a lot—otherwise I will look like a rabid dog who just ate something bloody—I brush my teeth with my power-sander (my sonic toothbrush) and GRIT (my toothpaste, which claims to reduce cavities—so I've only had eleven in the last six months).

I get two minutes before it automatically goes off, because I obviously don't know how long to brush my teeth. Two minutes doesn't seem long enough to kill all those mouth germs, so I take hold of my wand-like power toothbrush again and brush my teeth a second time. This time, using different toothpaste. This is an attempt to trick my teeth into not becoming complacent to one type of paste. I have applied this theory to my toothpaste and my sex life. Voila! Blood from my raw gums gushes out and there's that rabid dog look again.

Now I'm ready to kill some germs, so I rinse my mouth with a mouthwash that used to claim it killed germs—but now just kills the likelihood of a second date because it smells so foul—plus it kills my appetite (including sexual). My mouth tastes like the medicinal end of a doctor's needle, reminiscent of rubbing alcohol mixed with fear mixed with pain mixed with...blood from my gums! Finally, my breath is sterilized. And now my beard follicles should be nice and soft. Time to shave and sanitize my face. My new battery-operated Almost-Electric Shaver (renamed to protect the author) glides smoothly and nimbly across my face, removing hair stubble along with shaving cream. Afterward, I rinse the blade, put on more shaving cream, glide, rinse and repeat. After five minutes of this, all the while being careful not to cut myself, I rinse off the remaining shaving cream from my face, hoping throughout this tortuous ordeal that cutting off the hair at its roots will stop the damned stuff from growing back on my chinny-chin-chin. But it's a foolish thought; it always comes back.

Still not done, I apply astringent that smells like my medicinal mouthwash—to my entire face because it claims to reduce blackheads and pimples. At this point, I realize the number of times I accidentally nicked myself while shaving. The burn feels like a warm knife cutting through butter. No pain. No gain, I think. "Oh, this is agony!" I say. Now I know why women hate to shave and insist upon burning the stubble off with Nair®.

Speaking of women—I have puffy eyes, too. However, I don't like using products that cover up my problem areas. No eyeliner, tints, tattoos or glasses for me. Instead, I apply some Oil of Old Lady to lift and separate my eyes—so the crow's feet don't look like flat feet. Then I apply Retin A to make me feel young. The wrinkles don't go away, but I think—Hey, look at me, I can waste hundreds of dollars on a whim, just like when I was young and didn't understand the value of a dollar—Wow, I feel young. Hey, it works!

Lastly, I apply a musk-scented shaving balm to rid myself of those razor bumps (commonly known as "Pimples in Hiding"). Again, I feel the burn—but that's good, right? At least those gorgeous athletes claim it is.

After my blood-red face (burning does that) cools down, I spray some vanilla licorice cologne onto my chest, which smells good enough to eat—I hope. Finally, I swipe my underarms with the matching deodorant, which will be on the menu, too.

I know I'm done when I'm bleeding from every orifice (pores are orifices, aren't they?) My entire body and face feels like an acupuncturist's pincushion and I smell like a French whorehouse (so many scents, so little time).

So it goes every morning. And yet, I'm not done. Next, I must fix my hair. Where is my Rocky and Bullwinkle mousse? Should I use my ceiling fan, window fan or hand-fan to blow-dry my hair today? Use a brush, a comb, a pick, or just shave it all off? How about using my favorite brand of leave-in conditioner, GrowsHairBackOnMice Genitals tonic. It makes my scalp itch like something has been shaved off and has started growing back so surely it is working.

Or, should I mist it with my plant sprayer to keep it shiny (after all, it works on leaves)? Maybe, I should just start all over and dye it with RIT®. If I do that, I'll have to rework my face. Oh, well; such is the price of beauty—it's the price I pay for trying to reverse the aging process.

Just a Simple Bath

by Barbara Yohnka

There's nothing I like better than to run a warm bath, turn on the Jacuzzi® jets, and soak in a tub of effervescent, lavender-scented water. I can lay my head back and let the soothing, rhythmic waves de-stress my body and relax my mind.

I also like a shower, especially after working in the garden, having gotten two-year-old dirty, and letting the water cascade down my body like rain, making me feel as if I'm in an Amazonian waterfall. All I need is some Brazilian jazz to accompany my imaginary South American adventure.

Now, imagine what happens when you fracture an arm, for example. The bath, the place where you've spent countless hours, shampooing, rinsing, luxuriating, and yes, perhaps even playing with that special someone, becomes a terror more dreaded than Dante's final frigid level of Hell.

When I first broke my left forearm, not only was I in shock, but also in so much pain that neither bathing nor showering even crossed my mind. The medication made sure I didn't care. After a few days passed, the idea that I might actually have to go out in public looking and smelling like a homeless person after a dumpster dive, made me face the demon before me—the now-dreaded bathroom.

My cast covered my entire left arm from the knuckles to my armpit. It bent at the elbow so I looked like I was doing a bad imitation of Napoleon. I'd been wearing shorts and tank tops since the accident and it was with some consternation that I thought about not only what I would wear, but also how I would get it on my body. That was a challenge I'd have to face only after I had cleansed myself.

I started by running the bath water, thinking that if I filled it with several inches, I might safely get in and out of the tub, use a pitcher to wash and rinse my hair, and could slowly, if not effortlessly, wash the rest of my body without getting my cast anywhere near the water. In the diagram I'd drawn in my brain, I was as agile as a gazelle, having no difficulty stepping gingerly into the tub, and kneeling on the rubber mat, could maneuver, all with my right hand, the pitcher of water, the shampoo, conditioner, washcloth and body wash that would take me from an odoriferous invalid to a sweet-smelling member of society once again. Then I recalled that it was a trip over a sidewalk upheaval while walking my dog that had gotten me into this situation in the first place, so my confidence level took a bit of a hit.

I turned off the water, sat on the toilet and pondered the reality of my plight. I might be able to get in and out of the tub and remain standing but that made the distance between me and the water about five feet, not really close enough to do the job right. However, kneeling on the mat and getting up again without losing my balance might be difficult since my left arm was virtually useless and the pain medication had its side effects that needed to be factored into the equation.

The next thing I thought of was the order of activities in the bath. I usually turned on the water, waited for it to warm a little, stepped inside, wet my head, applied shampoo, then shaved under my arms while the fragrant cleanser did its job. I could still shave under my left arm although the cast's proximity to the pit area was a little too close for comfort. How would I shave my right armpit? I did a dry run and found that even the razor was too heavy for the swollen fingers of the left hand to hold and the position of the cast did not allow even a cursory swipe in the right armpit's direction.

Once I realized that I couldn't shave my right armpit, I also wondered how I would maneuver in the tub to shave my legs. It was June and the time of the year that legs became center stage. At the moment, my legs looked like they were covered with English moss. I might be able to genuflect on one knee in the tub and shave the other leg but I had the balance problem to deal with. Perhaps I'd look for that hair removal foam and that could solve all my leg-shaving problems.

I briefly considered throwing a plastic garbage bag over my arm and attempting to shower but the idea of anything more than air surrounding my wounded appendage was more than my low threshold of pain was willing to consider.

I finally opted to try a few inches of water in the tub. I brought my cordless phone into the bathroom for emergency purposes, filled the tub to ankle height and stepped inside. The water felt good on my feet and the thought of immersing another part of my tender body in the soothing water seemed orgasmic to me. I had gripped the right side of the tub, and knelt in the water when the phone rang. The shrill ring startled me and in turning to my left to grab it—momentarily forgetting I had a giant cast on my arm—I became unbalanced and slipped onto my left side, then wedged myself in the tub like Kirstie Alley trying to get into a size eight dress. My armpit rested on the tub's edge and fortunately, the cast portion had gotten nowhere near the water. However, while I was hyperventilating, attempting to right myself in the slippery porcelain, I breached the comfort zone between my pit and the casted area, and felt as if I'd gotten a porcelain "burn."

By this time, the phone had stopped ringing. In assessing my position—that of wounded creature in pain—I realized that all I had to do was get back into a kneeling position and I could right myself. Simple.

I couldn't grasp the right side of the tub ledge because

it was too slippery and now my left leg was awkwardly bent under my body and useless to me in trying to get my right leg into a kneeling position. I stopped, took a deep breath, looked around the tub area, and finally grabbed the faucet which gave me something sturdy to hold on to while I used my left hip to propel my body to the right, enabling me to maneuver the left leg out of its pinned position. In the meantime, I was able to kneel on the right, get the left knee in its position, spread the knees for balance and was finally ready to begin my bath.

Since several minutes had passed, the water was getting lukewarm so an infusion of hot water was required. That allowed me to scoot close to the faucet— which suddenly seemed off center—fill the pitcher, and begin the actual bathing process.

Feeling the water surround me, knowing that cleanliness was in my grasp, made shampooing and conditioning my hair, and rinsing the rest of my body, as much an accomplishment as parallel parking correctly for the first time. Feeling my legs immersed in the water, and seeing the hair on them looking much like seaweed in a shallow pond, made me want to go a step further in my cleansing process and attempt to shave my legs.

Since visualization is my key-learning tool, I pictured myself bringing the right knee up, with the foot firmly on the bath mat while the left leg held its position. I imagined grabbing the soap in my right hand, working it into a lather and applying it to my right leg. I surprised myself by actually executing my visualization and had begun the exciting process of shaving my leg.

With that leg fit for viewing, I handily switched legs, kneeling on the right, with the left foot gripping the mat. It was a little more difficult to reach the left side of the left leg, but after limbering up in the soothing water, I was able to accomplish my goal.

I thought it might be therapeutic to soak awhile so I turned the water on again to raise the water level. Resting my head on the back of the tub, I turned on the Jacuzzi jets since the water was now high enough to support their bursts. I was luxuriating in the bubbling water, soothing my stiff muscles, relaxing my back, closing my eyes and wishing I could dip even further below the water.

Apparently the combination of warm water and massaging jets, not to mention the residual painkillers, relaxed me to the point where I dozed off. Maybe only a few minutes had passed when I heard the dog bark, the phone ring, and the front door buzz all at the same time. Easily startled in my semi-conscious state, I slapped my right arm in the water as I struggled to extricate myself from the tub. But I was having difficulty. Somehow I had pushed the tub mat further into the water so my butt was on slick porcelain. Every time I tried to reach up to grab the faucet—which was considerably looser than before—I seemed to slip further. I was dangerously close to submerging my casted arm in the water.

I took a deep breath and had a thought that maybe my

omnipresent Border Collie, Maggie, could help me in some way, you know, like Lassie used to do. After seeing her chase her tail in excitement I realized that was one wish that would never come true.

I did actually have to get out of the tub, not only so I could find out who was calling and/or knocking, but also because I was becoming a prune.

Slowly I inched my way to a sitting position by using my feet to push my body towards the back of the tub. Once I was sitting up, I leaned over, grabbed the faucet handle, which scraped like a car door on a brick wall, and leveraged my left arm on the edge of the tub. After getting into a crouching position, I finally managed to stand up. Then the phone rang again, Maggie barked, the buzzer sounded.

Stepping out of the tub, I grabbed a nearby towel, wrapped it haphazardly around my head, threw on a terrycloth robe, stepped into my slippers, and opened the bathroom door. When I entered the sunny kitchen, I was scared shitless by cheers of "Surprise!" and surrounded by numerous friends and family.

"Were you in the tub?" my sister Norie asked, coming forward to hug me.

"What does it look like?" I said trying to put on my happy face, and wrinkling my nose to detect the smell of something edible in my house.

"I called twice," Cheri said, "then called Norie to meet me here to surprise you. I got a little worried when you didn't answer the phone so I called Diane to see if she had a key."

"I did but I couldn't find them," my friend Di said, "so I drove over and buzzed your door, then all your neighbors' doors because I couldn't remember who in your building had keys to your place."

"Then, while I was driving over, I called Rafael because I knew he definitely had keys to your place and he said he was planning to visit you anyway," Norie said.

Now I realized why Maggie was jumping up and down. I looked around and saw my two sisters, several friends, two neighbors, and the looks on their faces when they realized I had just been in the bath.

"You took a shower?" Cheri asked.

"No, a bath. I couldn't stand myself."

"So that's why you didn't answer the phone?" Norie queried.

"That would be why," I replied.

"So, in our efforts to surprise you, you scared the shit out of us," Rafael said. "You should've told us you were taking a bath so we didn't worry," he added, putting his arm around my shoulder. "Hmmm, you smell good."

"Thanks. What was I supposed to do? Text you? I didn't realize I couldn't bathe without your permission. Be glad I did. You wouldn't have wanted to be around me a little while ago," I said, smiling.

"Well, are we all gonna stand here or are we having pizza?" my neighbor Mary asked.

"And does anybody know where the paper plates are?"

"Pizza! That's what I smell! Good, all that bathing made me hungry," I said.

"I know where everything is," Rafael said. "I used to live here."

My sisters, Cheri and Norie flanked me. "So Barb, perhaps while we're here, we can help you do something with your hair."

The towel had fallen to my shoulders and except for smelling good, I looked like the wrath of God. "Sure, but no hard brushing; my head is sensitive."

"Give her another pain pill, Cheri, she'll be good to go," Norie laughed.

They both looked at me in my disheveled state, then we all started laughing.

"Could someone get me a slice of pizza?" I asked.

Section Three: Down the Drain with Style

From the Desk of Mr. Man-ners

Dear Mr. Man-ners:

I know that the toilet seat up or seat down is a question as ancient as "what came first, the chicken or the egg?" but I really want to know what you think. If you're a man, do you put the seat down after peeing, or not? While I have your attention, you might also answer another burning question; does the toilet paper roll go over or under when put on?

Needs to Know

Dear Needs to Know:

Since I am required as a man (thus the Mr.—Duh!) to lift the seat to pee, it's only fair that a woman be required to lower the seat to pee. What's fair for the goose is fair for the gander. It is definitely not fair for a man to have to lift the seat to pee then have to lower it so a woman can pee. Haven't you heard of equal rights? As to your second stupid question, since I live alone the over/under question isn't relevant. However, I'll give you an answer—the only true and relevant one—whichever way it ends up on the holder. Now I have a question for you: single or double-ply?

Mr. Man-ners

The Purrfect Murder

by Jennifer Djordjevic

People don't think cats can tell stories, but I'm setting the record straight by telling mine.

It begins in a shelter in the northwest suburbs of Chicago. The place had myriad cats running around on the day Simon and Lucy discovered me. The open playroom in the building featured cats and kittens stretching this way and that, preening, sleeping—waiting to be adopted by a loving couple or a family with kids yearning for a companion.

I wasn't among the hundreds in the playroom, but rather tucked away in a crate in another section of the shelter. There were other cats there too—separated because they'd just been neutered or because they didn't fit the social profile the facility demanded. I know why I was locked away but I doubted Simon and Lucy would be told.

*   *   *

Those two idiots should have known I wasn't quite right from the beginning. I tried to warn them from the moment the shelter volunteer pried me from the rancid crate I'd been kept in for the last 73 days. I desperately tried to grab the edges of the door as the volunteer's meaty hands wrapped around my midsection. My paws weren't strong enough and my nails did me no good. My previous owners had considered removing them after I scratched a two-inch gash across their daughter's face, but the animal-loving vet convinced them otherwise.

"It's really inhumane," the vet had said. "It's like removing the tips of your fingers up to the first knuckle." My former owners argued for 20 minutes before deciding to let my transgressions slide one last time.

Oblivious of my past misdeeds Simon and Lucy greeted me with wide grins when the volunteer turned around. "Oh how cute is she," Lucy squealed. The volunteer placed me in her lap and waited for a reaction. I tried my best to sway their opinion of me by acting cold and disinterested. I shied away at Simon's touch and growled deeply when Lucy got her face too close to mine.

"Not very friendly," Simon said taking his hand away. He looked at his watch, slid his hand into a waiting black glove and tightened the scarf around his neck.

"Ah, come on," Lucy said in a sugary voice. "She is soooo cute. She just needs some love and attention."

Thirty minutes later, much to my dismay, I was packed in an open-topped box with a tattered rag and toy mouse with both plastic eyes missing. A small plastic bag, bulging with cat food samples and a "report card" of when my next vaccinations were due, was tossed beside me.

*   *   *

I was 20-something days into my new life when I started to understand Lucy and Simon's schedules. Monday through Friday Lucy worked. She woke most days at 5 a.m., bounced around to a workout video until 6 a.m. and then showered, dressed, applied make-up and left. She always returned at 6:30 p.m.—no earlier, no later.

Simon was different. He slept until his internal clock woke him up. Sometimes it was 10, other times it was noon. There was no rhyme or reason to his sleep patterns. Simon's cell phone always rang around 9:30 to no avail. One thing was for certain, he was always up and out of the house by 12:45. He either worked outside or left for his job in the city.

Each of them had a separate bathroom. Lucy's was upstairs and Simon's was downstairs. Both were kept very differently. Lucy hated me in her bathroom. She would enter, shoo me out and shut the door in my face. Occasionally, when she was in a good mood, Lucy would run the cold water in the sink and let me sip for a few moments.

Simon's bathroom, just off the foyer, on the lower level, was open at all times. When Lucy was gone he'd do his business without shutting the door. Occasionally, I gazed in, uninterested in what he was doing, waiting for the moment he'd turn the water on or flush the toilet. This excited me. I was curious about the rushing, swirling water. Where did it go and how did the bowl fill back up? Simon always left the seat up which gave me the perfect opportunity to jump on the rim and peer down into the bowl as the water was sucked down and away.

In addition to my bathroom antics, I had taken a liking to scratching anything to annoy them. The days Simon worked away from home were ideal. This was my time to lounge, scratch and jump without getting a face full of water from the spray bottle they used to discipline me. Mostly, I scratched the carpet on the stairs but then took to the leather couches and the dining room table. I felt a deep sense of accomplishment the first time Simon complained.

"Lucy, this is getting ridiculous. Do you see what this cat is doing to our furniture?" Simon whined. "I can't take it anymore."

"I know it's annoying," said Lucy. "But remember what the shelter said. It's going to take a while for her to get used to the house and used to us. She was abused, remember?"

"Okay, but enough is enough. Maybe we should just get her claws removed." Simon suggested.

"Nope, not doing that," said Lucy firmly. "I don't care how much she scratches. We rescued her and now you want to torture her by removing her claws?"

"I'm not saying—you know what? Never mind. But if she gets into my watch collection and does something to it then we're going to have a problem," Simon said, making one final point.

I watched the transaction gleefully from my hiding spot under the credenza in the living room. Simon would never win, I knew that for sure. It gave me a new sense of power like none I'd ever felt before.

*   *   *

Fifty-three days in was a Monday. I'd just got finished scratching the dining room wallpaper when I heard the front door open. I knew something wasn't right. Glancing at the clock I noticed the hands weren't in the correct positions for Lucy to be home yet. It was only 5 p.m.

"I'm so excited," a muffled voice said. "I can't believe we're getting her tonight."

Lucy and Simon walked around the corner taking off their coats as they talked.

"I'm glad we're getting one that isn't from a shelter," Simon said.

My ears perked up instantly. What one? What were they discussing?

"I know, Meow Meow is fine but she's so shy and not very friendly. I think a new kitten might bring out another side of her. What do you think?" Lucy questioned. "It will be great to see them together." A jolt of panic ran down my spine. A kitten? That would never do.

Several hours later, Simon and Lucy donned their jackets and walked out the door. Suspecting where they were going sent me into a scratching frenzy. A new kitten meant trouble. They were needy, whiny and hungry. They'd also be curious, traipsing over my territory. They'd become the "favorite" and take up all of Simon's and Lucy's time.

Enraged I started with the Berber on the stairs and made my way down to the loveseat in the living room. I even managed to tear down the shower curtain in Simon's bathroom before I could calm myself down enough to figure out what I was going to do. They'd be back eventually and I needed a plan.

Nearly three hours later, the human traitors entered the house with their new "friend." The "thing," as I decided to call it, was tucked away in a lidded FedEx box probably filled with the same items I was brought home with.

Without removing her coat or shoes, Lucy took the box from Simon and placed it on the couch. Sitting beside it, she gingerly lifted the box and peered inside. A wide smile grew across her face and she turned to Simon.

"You have to see this. She is so cute. Her little head is curled up under her paw." Lucy opened the box top a bit further so Simon could look.

I could feel a hairball inching up my throat. God, they were pathetic. Didn't they even see me? I'm right here I wanted to meow! Right here, under the couch. I've been in this house for nearly two months and you don't even want me!

The next morning Lucy was up early. "Meow Meow," she called, waiting for me to scamper up the stairs and rub my soft fur against her bare legs. "Meow Meow—where are you?" As I rounded the corner from the lower level my heart sank. Lucy, in pink shorts and a white tank top, was standing in the hallway at the top of the stairs. I knew what she wanted. She wanted to introduce me to The Thing.

I slowed my pace and slunk the rest of the way up the stairs. Lucy kneeled down and attempted to grab me around the waist. I was having none of it. I nipped at her fingers causing her to jolt and nearly fall backwards.

"Meow, stop it!" Her voice elevated to a harsh whisper. "You're going to have to learn to like the new kitten. I'm sorry, but that's it." She stood up and walked over to the bathroom looking over her shoulder. "Come here. Come on, Sweetie." Her voice had taken on a sugary quality.

I moved closer, more curious than anything. I needed to know who my rival was. I needed to know whom I was going to maim, possibly kill. Information was power. I wasn't about to let my pride and anger get in the way of learning as much about this new interloper as I could.

Feigning excitement, I perked up and rushed towards the open bathroom door. I could smell The Thing before I even saw the box. Having been cramped up for a night in a dark enclosure with no food must have been horrible. I smiled at the thought.

To my dismay, the scene I was presented with was hardly one of discomfort. Before retiring to bed, Lucy and Simon had brought up a large metal crate for the new kitten to stretch out in. To comfort her, they'd lined it with soft old T-shirts and tossed in a fuzzy, albeit tattered, stuffed bear. A matching set of bowls sat side by side. One with fresh water and the other with goldfish shaped pellets that smelled divine.

Lucy stood to the side as I cautiously moved forward to inspect the intruder. "Heeeeeeeeeeeeeeeeeeee! Grrrrrrr." A hiss and a low growl instinctively escaped my lips. The hair stood up over my entire body and my tail went rigid. I stopped short of the cage and waited for a response.

From under the warm T-shirts emerged a tiny smoke grey kitten—about the size of a squirrel. Its face was comprised of a thin white strip of fur from the crown of its head to the tip of its nose. Interested, large eyes stared at me through the crate bars. Each foot, save one, were also white, as if the kitten was given a pair of white socks and had stupidly lost one along the way.

"Mew" was all it said.

I retreated backwards while looking up at Lucy, then back at the kitten, returning my glance to Lucy once more. What did she expect of me? Did she expect me to warmly welcome this revolting bag of grey-covered fur and flesh?

"Aw, come on, Meow," Lucy said, sitting on the edge of the tub and reaching down to pat me on the head. "You'll be fine and you'll love Trixie." Ugh. Trixie. So that was the rodent's name.

Several days later my feelings about Trixie hadn't changed. Simon and Lucy had decided to keep her in the bathroom so they could strategically manage the interactions between us. Not that I was interested in seeing The Thing each day but I needed to know the lay of the land.

I was plotting to kill Trixie.

The idea to snuff out the new kitten came before the day she arrived. I'm a loner. I don't do well with other cats. Never have, never will. This is what the shelter didn't tell Simon and Lucy. What they didn't write down in my report card was that I was responsible for the deaths of several cats and kittens years earlier.

My first kill wasn't intentional. I had just turned one year old when my previous owners brought home a much older cat from a local shelter. For two weeks they kept the cat in the downstairs bathroom, occasionally giving me the chance to sneak in and sniff around.

As the separation period neared an end, they left the door open and no longer supervised my visits. On the day the new cat was to be let out of its cage, I sauntered into the bathroom, noticed a wire hanger lying on the floor and decided it would be the perfect plaything for the newbie and me. With much enthusiasm I pushed the hanger over to the cage and flicked it up against the metal, jolting the cat out of its slumber.

It did the trick and within moments the two of us where passing the hanger back and forth, both of us delighted at the racket we were making.

The accident happened with a flick of my paw. As I swatted the hanger back in the newcomer's direction, the curved hook entered the cage and somehow penetrated the cat's cheek and eye before coming out its nostril. The cat yanked and pulled desperately trying to free itself from the large hook. The struggle increased the damage and eventually the cat bled to death. At first I was shocked at the brutality. But somewhere in my walnut-sized brain I was comforted knowing I would no longer have to compete for my owner's attention. From that moment, the thought of killing became exciting.

My second murder was much different. I schemed and I plotted. I knew what I was going to do and how I was going to get away with it. I made sure my second set of owners thought the kitten had died of accidental suffocation. They found it in the bathroom, lying soundlessly on the rug in front of the shower, curled up under the shower curtain, which had been ripped off the hooks that held it in place. They had no clue that I had lured the kitten in, pretending I was going to show it how to drink out of the toilet.

Once inside the bathroom, I pounced. We wrestled on the floor. I had a hard time keeping my claws sheathed, but I knew I'd be found out if the kitten was injured. In one swoop I yanked down the plastic shower curtain lining down and buried the kitten inside.

Its tiny face peered up at me helplessly, two little paws next to its cheeks, begging to be let out. I looked away and used my weight to keep the kitten from moving. Eventually, my prey stopped breathing and my work was done. The great part was that there was no clean up. My paws weren't dirty since I used my weight to hold down the plastic. It was a clean kill.

Murder became easy after this incident. I enjoyed the chase, the entrapment and the kill. Three kittens were drowned, two were electrocuted and one was mauled by its own claws and left to die in the toilet. That was a tricky one. My last job, before moving in with Simon and Lucy, was logistically astounding if I do say so myself. It involved a good-for-nothing Golden Retriever, catnip and a bottle of Valium® my owners had left out.

Now that I had a new nemesis, it was time to revisit my former skills and take out this new threat. Shaking myself from a pleasant reverie late, I decided that today, day 65 of my residence, was as good a day as any to hatch my next plan. It was a Monday and Lucy would be up and gone by 6:15. It had only been a few days since Trixie had been allowed out of her crate. Lucy and Simon decided she'd been "fully integrated" and would be fine to wander the house without restraint.

I wasn't worried about Simon. He'd probably sleep until noon, as was his usual pattern. Just in case, I decided to get to work early. The extra time would give me a chance to do things correctly so everything went right and to allow for any clean up that might be necessary.

At 6:50, I swung into action. Trixie was downstairs on the first level exploring her new world and traipsing all over my territory. She used my litter box and drank my water. My food was now her food. I was disgruntled and disturbed to have been forced to eat and drink out of the same bowls, but nobody had asked my opinion. I reminded myself that the situation would be short-lived.

Once on the lower level, I moved stealthily to Simon's bathroom. The place was in typical fashion. Clothes were strewn about and the toilet seat was up. The bathroom smelled of soap, musky cologne and toothpaste. I scanned the small room and determined the ideal spot for this morning's murder.

Trixie was eating when I came out of the bathroom. It was 7:30 and I needed to move things along. Despite a small amount of discomfort, I approached Trixie as if I wanted to play with her.

The dumb bag of bones took the bait and jumped forward and back, teasing me into pouncing. I played the game. We rolled on the floor in the kitchen for a bit and then moved into the living room. We were getting closer to the bathroom by the second.

I attempted to move into the bathroom, but Trixie was having none of it. She had tired of playing and wasn't in the mood to explore Simon's space. A tinge of panic set in but dissipated just as fast—I knew exactly what to do. With Trixie in sight, I moved towards the toilet and jumped onto the rim.

I would show her how great it was to drink out of the bowl.

Falling for the old trick, she entered the bathroom and sniffed her way towards me. I turned and gazed into the toilet. I wanted to play out the act for full effect.

Oh, God. Simon hadn't flushed. A shiver of disgust jolted through my spine. It's just an act, it's just an act, I thought, wrinkling up my face as I leaned forward, using my peripheral vision to my advantage.

Trixie was fascinated. She moved closer and closer until she was nearly up against the pot itself.

As if on cue, she stood on her hind legs and pulled herself up so she, too, could look inside the bowl to see what was so interesting. The timing was perfect.

I pulled myself away from the open bowl and sprung from the rim to the bathroom door. Trixie, looking uneasy, darted her eyes from left to right. She eased a little—probably thinking I was ready to play again.

But I wasn't in the mood to play. Using my left hind leg to shut the bathroom door—the entire time keeping a steady eye on Trixie—I enjoyed this moment of victory to the fullest. A Cheshire grin spread across my face and tickled my whiskers. I was good. I was very good at this.

There would be no going back now.

Death by Plunger: A Christina DeNucci Murder Mystery

by Gail Cohen

1—No "Jokes for the John" Here

When Lieutenant Christina DeNucci found the female victim lying face up with a plunger jammed against her face, her first reaction was to laugh out loud.

"Jeez, Lieutenant," Joey Archer, the beat cop keeping watch over the crime scene uttered, "have some respect."

DeNucci tried to wipe the smile from her face, thankful no civilians were around to see what even she would call an inappropriate reaction to a death scene.

Frankly, given the bizarre nature of the weapon, looking serious would be a Herculean feat. All of the training literature on the planet couldn't have prepared the 27-year-old investigator for the experience of finding a shapely, nude woman wedged between a toilet and tub with a Lucite®-handled rubber plunger straddling her cheekbones.

"You've gotta admit this is one strange crime scene,

Archer," she added, focusing her eyes on the woman's face so the young cop couldn't see the slight smirk that lingered. "The bacteria on that plunger alone could have done the job without the added pressure of the suction cup."

Careful to avoid contaminating anything, she put on a pair of paper booties and spent a couple of minutes getting the lay of the land before her ruminations were disrupted by a shout from Archer. "Lieutenant, the crime scene techs are here."

DeNucci backed out of the small bathroom to make room for forensics. Two investigators carried metal and plastic gearboxes and digital cameras. They immediately began discussing how to reconnoiter and evaluate the body in the small space, and then started removing the swabs, sprays, tapes and chemicals needed to sleuth out invisible clues.

While they worked, DeNucci's eyes swept the adjoining room, taking in details of the neat bedroom. "A woman who makes her bed even before she's had time to shower," she mused, using a gloved hand to pull back a small section of bed linen. Next, she began picking up and re-depositing framed photos, examined a hardbound copy of a best-selling novel and checked the surface of the dainty bedside clock ticking away in its porcelain case.

"No dust," she mumbled, making the classic finger-sweep test mothers-in-law have applied to surfaces for generations. "Perfect body and it looks like she had enough sense to prioritize her time by hiring a housekeeper," she concluded.

Archer interrupted the detective's thoughts. "Want to know the victim's name?"

"Sure."

"Giselle," he read from a small note pad, pronouncing it Guess-ell.

"Giselle," DeNucci corrected him. "It's French. Last name?"

"Caron," he replied slowly, wanting to get the surname right.

"You're joking!"

Archer shrugged, his face a blank.

DeNucci walked back to the bathroom and peered in. "I should have recognized that face—even with a plunger over it. Archer, you're in the presence of a famous cadaver. This girl's a TV celeb. She hands over cash to contestants on a daytime game show called 'Show Me Yours and I'll Show You Mine.' Jesus. Giselle Caron," her voice trailed off as she pulled out her cell phone, turned away from the bathroom and began pushing buttons.

"Hey, Jess. I need to speak to the chief. We're going to have a media circus on our hands with this one," she said quietly, walking around the room. "The body belongs to Giselle Caron. The cash girl on that daytime TV game show." The detective paused a moment but continued to poke into drawers and examine trinkets with her gloved hand.

"For cryin' out loud, Chief," she said after a long silence, "I can't believe you don't know who she is. Call your wife. She'll know. Better send someone from communications over here fast. We'll need a talking head."

She peered behind a Roman shade-covered window. "Make it soon. I see media on the street already."

While an expanding team of investigators did their respective jobs, DeNucci completed the requisite space canvas. A self-proclaimed slob—and proud of it—she nevertheless stood in awe of the luxury apartment's orderliness. The thought may have triggered a psychic vibration. Next thing she knew, a howl went up from the front door.

A woman, dressed in a maid's uniform, dropped a massive, commercial vacuum on Joey Archer's toes as he attempted to block her entry. Uttering a string of unintelligible words in Spanish, the maid broke through when the cop grabbed for his throbbing foot.

DeNucci took the woman's arm and led her to a stylish red couch, leaving Archer to deal with his injured toe and the Hoover®. She delivered the news of Caron's death gently.

"You work for Ms. Caron?" She asked.

"Si. I come every day. I clean every day," she added.

"I'm Christina DeNucci," she said, "I'm the lead detective on this case." She handed the maid a business card from her jacket pocket, took out a notebook and began to scribble notes. "I need to ask you some questions. First, can I have your name?"

"Lourdes. Lourdes Gonzales."

"How long have you worked for Ms. Caron?"

"Four years. She pay me to come every day and clean. Sometimes, there's no thing to clean but I come and scrub anyway."

"Can you tell me a little about her?" DeNucci had developed the habit of nodding at the same time she took notes. The head bob helped keep suspects talking.

"She like to have every little thing perfect. Mucho perfect. She even make the husband crazy. Not husband; ex-husband. He no like things so perfect."

"His name?"

"Senor Caron."

"First name?"

"Stefan. He work with her. On her show." She pronounced the word cho.

"Girlfriends?"

"Mucho men friends. No girlfriend that I see."

"Parents?"

"Si," Lourdes said, incredulous. "Everybody have parents. That is how we are born."

"Are they alive?"

"She no talk about parents."

The detective asked the maid to inspect a wall of photos. "Have you seen or met any of these people?"

"No. I am here in the morning and the Signora Caron has gone to work, so I be alone."

Half an hour of pointed questioning brought no revelations so DeNucci dismissed her with a warning that she wasn't to leave town.

"Where I going?" she asked.

When DeNucci didn't respond, Lourdes shrugged and headed to the door, glaring daggers at Joey Archer. She snatched the vacuum and left, Hoover® Wind Tunnel™ in tow.

Nearly a full day of wandering Caron's home in search of leads proved fruitful. DeNucci came away with bank records, a phone directory, laptop computer and half-a-dozen snail mail death threats from an angry fan.

Canvassing the building wasn't as productive. Folks fell into three camps: Nobody home, home but no idea who lived in Caron's unit and a couple of Chatty Cathys who watched too much CSI and offered their theories on why the "rude and haughty" woman had been killed. One said she wouldn't watch the game show if someone put a gun to her head.

2—Louis, Haul in the Usual Suspects

Christina DeNucci had an inordinate ability to coordinate her data gathering within the same time frame as the forensics crew. Today was no exception. She finished just as a gurney bearing the zippered, black body bag was wheeled toward the elevator for transport to the coroner's office. The last thing DeNucci saw was the Lucite plunger handle poking from the black bag. It looked like a long, skinny, clear erection.

Once the gurney cleared the elevator doors, the detective turned to Archer. He was still nursing a sore foot and limped as he yellow-taped the door to preserve the crime scene. She waved, and then headed for her car and home.

DeNucci may have been a self-admitted slob but, as everyone in her squad agreed, her investigational methods were organizationally brilliant. That's what earned her lieutenant's stripes at such an early age. True, she was obsessive. But that made her meticulous. She rarely missed a detail, so when she headed out the following morning, it was with a specific agenda: Checking out Stefan Caron at his WSSN-TV offices.

The title on his door read Producer. He was nice looking and had a strong handshake.

"I'm sorry for your loss," she offered after introducing herself.

"Thanks," he answered. "I've been trying to figure out who might have done this, but I'm stumped." He was frank and direct while detailing his brief, tumultuous marriage to the deceased. He called the pairing a "major mistake of epic proportions driven by hormones and the glamour of the industry." Caron effortlessly answered all questions put to him without losing eye contact.

If he's got anything to hide, the detective thought, he's doing a yeoman job of acting.

DeNucci thanked him and handed him a business card. She refused his offer to escort her to the door, following the corridor he pointed out. Along the route, she was stopped by a loud "Psst" coming from an office near the entrance.

"You the cop on the Caron case?" the young woman asked, waving her in, then shutting the door. "You didn't hear it from me, but those two had a big fight the other day," she confided. "We hear every word around here. Stefan said he'd kill her if she didn't stop meddling in his affairs."

"Your name?"

"Tracy. I'm a production assistant on her show."

"Tracy what?"

"Do you really need to know? I don't want this getting out."

"I'd say six people saw you wave me in here. This place isn't exactly a model for offices stressing privacy," the detective explained.

"Taylor. Tracy Taylor."

"Any idea why he was threatening her?"

"That woman was a total head case. Conceited. Arrogant. She has—had—a lot of power and she knew how to use it. There aren't many Giselle Caron fans here," Taylor added.

Three pages of notes later, DeNucci decided she had enough. She thanked Taylor and left, intent on heading directly to the precinct. On the way, she rang the medical examiner's office to see if any of the evidence gathered by the forensics team had been processed.

A lab tech answered the phone and delivered bad news. "Bodies are stacked up like planes at JFK the day before Christmas," she reported. "You'll have to take a number." She hung up without saying another word.

Once she reached her desk, DeNucci went into automatic mode. An admitted technophile when she needed to be, the detective had serious respect for the time the Internet and e-records saved her on background checks. But when it came to good old-fashioned methodology, she'd take a telephone any day. First up, she sorted highlighted notes taken over the past 24 hours. Then she retrieved a plastic bag taken from the crime scene.

DeNucci found it odd but fortuitous to have, in her gloved hands, an organized list of Giselle's contacts. Some days, it felt as though everyone on the planet was using a cell or Blackberry to store data, but the late Ms. Caron must have had reservations about the safety of electronic storage. Knowing the directory would be a gold mine of data, she failed to turn the book in with the other evidence. Now, she discreetly replicated pages on a cranky, old copier before walking the directory to the evidence room with an apology.

This had been a risky move, but occasionally DeNucci did an end run around rules. Should the book be challenged in court, it would be noted that it had been returned late and she could be in for a reprimand. For now, she was willing to take that chance. She handled the situation with apologies, then returned to her desk to begin making calls.

By midnight, both ears numb from the pressure of the handset, she scanned dozens of pages of notes and composed a summary list:

—3 people in building know and dislike GC; can't recall last time they talked to vic.

—Production asst Taylor says hubby a likely candidate after fight (see notes).

May be payback. Taylor had recent fling with him.

—Receptionist confirms prod. asst. slept with SC; he recently started seeing intern. Still bitter? Motive to frame him?

—1 sister w/ French name (Dominique sp?) lives in Memphis TN; claims they've been estranged 4 years. Says "dump body in a tar pit; she doesn't care." In TN day of murder. TB conf.

—Financial mgr. Frank Olsen not grieving over vic's death; will contact lawyer re: disposition of will.

—Call lawyer AM to see who inherits; at Bar Assoc. dinner t'nite.

DeNucci had also called Giselle's gynecologist, three males (two, she discovered, had wives), the station manager, her agent, folks at three neighborhood pizza joints and several Chinese take-out restaurants. She left the precinct building knowing more about the people who hated her than any other victim she could recall.

48 hours. They say that's the lynchpin for solving

crimes. After that, cases go colder than winter in Chicago.

"Shit," the detective said as she started her car. On the seat beside her, a forgotten list jolted her mind from the case. "I didn't get cat food." She wasn't in the mood to shop, but the convenience store would serve her needs, so she forked over twice the usual cash for a bag of generic kibble and headed home. At least the boys would be happy.

3—Double the Body Count; Film at Eleven

Still angry about the high price of cat food at convenience stores, the detective didn't so much walk into the precinct the next day as she stormed in. DeNucci hated to be looking at day three with so little material to work with. She decided to visit the Evidence Room and retrieve the hate mail Caron had stashed neatly in a desk drawer.

She also got the victim's lawyer on the phone and was delighted to learn she could see him within the hour. She flew out the door and headed for her car—only to find that it had been haphazardly decorated with rolls of white bath tissue.

"Assholes!" she screamed aloud to nobody in particular. "When I find out who did this, I'll..." she stopped. I'll what, she thought? She continued mumbling as she peeled back and crumpled up streamers, muttering under her breath.

Once the car looked acceptable, she hopped in and took

off, the vehicle spewing squares and clumps of paper. She had no idea that a paper trail billowed from her car's rear courtesy of a roll that had been tucked under her bumper. It continued to dispense a stream of white in its wake.

By the time she reached the firm of Olson, Scott and Schwartz, DeNucci had to take a deep breath to collect her composure. Her pulse had been racing as her mind tried to ID the toilet paper culprit. A reflection of her image in an ornate lobby mirror looked harried and askance, so she took a few breaths and let them out before facing the lawyer.

The detective's hopes were dashed just minutes into her interview. Caron's attorney invoked client privilege and could only say that the will left all of the woman's resources to a charity called Third World Children.

"Figures," the detective said aloud as she left the building empty-handed. "The woman would never allow a child to contaminate her perfect condo, but she'll underwrite some rice." Her cell phone interrupted the mean-spirited rumination. "Talk to me, Doc."

"Detective," the medical examiner started as DeNucci crossed the street to her car, "You...like this."

"I'm not liking anything today so you may as well be the exception," she answered.

"No, I said you won't like this. Damn cell phones. Nothing to report. Healthy, attractive woman dead due to asphyxiation. The plunger head was the biggest I've ever seen. The cleanest, too. No prints. Too bad. Lucite and rubber are great surfaces," he added.

DeNucci pulled open her car door, "Thanks," she said as the beep indicating another call sounded, "for nothing." She pushed a button to pick up the second call. "DeNucci."

"We've got another one." It was the chief's voice. One-of-a-kind. Unmistakable timbre. "Get over there. I've already called the PR guy."

DeNucci scribbled the address on a burger wrapper lying on the floor of her car, then popped the transmission into gear. When she arrived at the elegant, gated villa, several reporters had already staked out territory on the street. You've gotta hand it to them, she thought. Nothing like a police scanner to keep reporters on top of things.

Her vehicle, with its temporary warning light fixture half-heartedly slapped onto its roof, was waved in by a beat cop who noticed flecks of toilet paper still adhering to the car's body. He had the good sense not to mention them when he glimpsed her face.

Threading her way into the interior of the estate, DeNucci expected a body immediately, but nary a person was to be found in the expansive great room introducing this House Beautiful-worthy residence. The place was massive—not just in size but scale and layout. She followed voices back to a bedroom.

"Déjà vu," said Archer, who stood beside an open glass door that led into what appeared to be an adjoining bathroom. DeNucci was immediately thankful for the room's size. After squeezing into typical bathrooms, most the size of phone booths, this one would be a breeze to maneuver around. She made her way to the glass shower stall.

"Is this a joke?" she asked, turning to Archer.

"Whatever."

The nude male body was soaked, thin and aging. "Plumbing isn't meant to bear this kind of weight," she observed, sticking a gloved finger into the length of standard clothesline rope that secured him neatly to the protruding metal piping. The bulk of the squeaky-clean corpse had pulled the showerhead out at least six inches. Only quality construction kept the entire pipe from destroying the tiled wall.

Plaster and ceramic pieces of various sizes littered the shower floor. Some stuck to the deceased, making him look like a Christmas tree trimmed with ornaments.

"Who's this nice, clean soul?" she asked.

"Roberto Salazar. Did I pronounce it right?" he asked with a touch of sarcasm.

"The architect? Guess it's not kosher to have money and power these days," she said, admiring the stylish bathroom that had witnessed the demise of one of the city's most controversial building designers.

"You know him, too?"

"Archer—don't you read the paper?" She stepped out of the bathroom and began perusing the bedroom with its ceiling murals, tapestry window treatments and

European-styled furniture. Nothing appeared out-of-place.

Like Caron's gallery, walls filled with photos showed Salazar up-close and personal with recognizable movers and shakers. It would be hard to guess whom among the rich and famous wasn't represented. The detective sighed as she swept the room from left to right with her eyes.

Methodically, DeNucci began going through drawers, closets, desks and cabinets. To her surprise, she discovered that Salazar, like Caron, also had an aversion to technology. His studio held huge numbers of drafting and legal pads overflowing with hand-written notes.

In his home studio, voluminous file cabinets were stuffed with yellow, hand-written communications and drawings tucked into folders. She was methodically going through some when Archer escorted a young man into the office.

"Says he works for Salazar," he said, looking down at his note pad. "Benito Salazar."

"Mr. Salazar, I'm Detective DeNucci. Sorry for your loss," she looked at him. "Let's start with the obvious. Are you related?" she said.

"He's my father," the emotionless young man responded.

"You said you worked for him," Archer said defensively.

"I do. He was my father and my boss," the young man said. "More so the second," he added with no emotion.

"Can you tell me about your father?" the detective asked.

"What can I tell you that hasn't hit the papers?" Benito asked. "Born and raised in Spain. Came to the U.S. as a penniless boy to make his dream of becoming the Michelangelo of architecture come true. He was determined to out-Wright Frank Lloyd Wright," he added. The flatness in his voice added confirmation that there was no love lost between the two.

"You an only child?"

"No," he responded, "there were six of us to ignore growing up."

"Do your siblings work for him, too?"

"Hardly. I'm the only one who wanted to design buildings badly enough to stick around. Maybe I wanted to see if that would get his attention," said Benito, coldness in his voice that isn't usually associated with a child encountering a dead parent. "Can I see him? I just want to make sure he's really dead and that this isn't a dream."

"You'll have to wait until the room is secured by the forensics people," she said, getting back to her questions. "Can you think of anyone who might want your father dead?"

"I can't think of anyone who would want him alive," he responded. "My brothers and sisters have all moved away," Benito injected, reminded of the question DeNucci had posed about his siblings moments earlier. "I stuck around to jump-start my career. I had planned to leave my father's firm as soon as I had enough experience and clients. Guess I'll stick around now," he added.

"You get the business?"

"Get serious. The old man wasn't that generous. I just don't have to escape him by relocating now," Benito explained. "I'm free."

4—And Body Makes Three

After spending nearly the entire day at the Salazar home, DeNucci came away with a short list of potential suspects. Benito had been a font of information, helping cull pertinent facts from hand-written documents. He seemed eager to help, but remained as emotionally off-putting as he had when he got the news of his father's death.

Once he completed answering all of the questions the detective posed, Benito decided he could do nothing more and realized he really had no desire to see the body. He'd do that at the funeral. He wanted to go back to work.

It was obvious that Junior was overjoyed to be out from under his father's shadow and DeNucci quickly learned why. Not only was Senior impossible to get along with, but he wouldn't let the young architect work with computer programs he had been trained to use. That meant Benito had to hand-draw everything, then transfer it to the computer.

Now that he no longer had to take the double route, he

was eager to get moving, but no amount of pleading got him into his father's offices to retrieve client files. "Once the house is clear, I'll give you a call," DeNucci promised. Benito left empty handed.

Once the body had been bagged and tagged, it was again time for Archer to do his taping routine. The last piece of yellow plastic secured, they locked the house, headed for their cars and vacated the scene.

It was late. DeNucci intended to stop off at the precinct just long enough to check in before going home. But when she perused her desk, she decided it held too much to face in the morning. She shuffled through phone messages and tapped on her e-mail icon. The long list of messages was more than she could deal with.

Keys in hand, she said "Enough" and turned out the desk lamp. She nearly ran into Sarah Jessup, one of the few other female detectives on staff.

"Hear you're working the Doo-Doo Doer," Sarah laughed.

"The Doo-Doo Doer? Wait a minute. Did you TP my car yesterday?" she asked.

Sarah shrugged noncommittally, "Do I behave in such juvenile ways?"

"Any chance it could be Archer? He lectured me on my behavior at the Caron scene. Frankly, I can't think of a more undignified place to die."

Sarah nodded her head in agreement. "Got plans?"

"For tonight?"

"No, next week. Of course, tonight. Want to get a drink?" Jessup asked.

"That's not just the best idea I've heard today but the most sane. Girl, you can't even imagine how awful Salazar looked hanging from that showerhead, all wet, soggy and wrinkled." The detectives automatically turned left in unison as DeNucci continued. "And the only Salazar kid— who worked with his dad, but the way—didn't shed a tear for his old man. Cold. Really cold."

The Sixty-Ninth Precinct, a bar that had served as home to four generations of police professionals, was best known for serving doubles to cops and exhibiting precinct photos on every available surface. At the entrance, portraits of officers serving in the 1930's began a pictorial timeline that stretched across one wall.

Portraits of officers who had died or been killed in the line of duty were hung with ribbons. A large, blue bar with a long line of stools—some with brass tags bearing the names of select legends—dominated the other wall.

"Any thoughts on the perpetrators?" Sarah asked after drinks were ordered.

"Honestly, Caron and Salazar moved in different circles. He was 63. She was 36. The transposition of their ages is as close as I can get to connecting 'em so far. Salazar's kid checks out. Neither of the vics should ever have been considered for ambassadorships. I haven't found anyone who liked either one."

"Are you thinking these are isolated incidents?"

"I don't know what to think. Two universally disliked rich people put down in two bathrooms in three days is a bit too coincidental."

Sarah downed a shot and concentrated a moment on her tall glass of beer. "Have you pulled phone records to see if there was any contact between 'em?" she asked.

"I've already put in a request and since the media is breathing down the boss's neck, I'm sure I'll get it fast. You know, Sarah, I spent a day at each crime scene and I've gotta tell you, neither of these characters seem to have left behind anyone ready to shed a tear. I'm thinking both funerals are going to be conducted in empty churches."

The women exhausted the topic of the murders and moved on to personal matters. Both were committed to hiding their "girly sides" to avoid ribbing from the guys on the squad, but infrequent escapes to a spa offered them a chance to get to know each other pretty well. This impromptu stop required no catch-up time.

They split up and headed in different directions. DeNucci was relieved to find nothing on her car. She had become paranoid since the papering incident and approached parking lots with a touch of trepidation. If she hadn't been so damned busy with her cases, she might have gathered the tissue into evidence bags and tried to find the artist.

DeNucci started her car and headed into the night. She spent the ride home mentally seeking match-ups on the Caron and Salazar crime scenes. Even with a couple of drinks under her belt, nothing came together, but at least she fell asleep quickly. It could have been a blissful night had ringing bells not awakened her.

Thinking it was her alarm, she used her fist to hit the snooze button, but the ringing persisted. It dawned on her that it was her phone; not the alarm.

"Turn off your cell?" Archer's somewhat groggy voice asked.

"Oh, Jesus, what now?" Middle-of-the-night calls were never good news.

"Got a tub floater this time," he said. "And I actually know her. You may want to call the chief and give him the good news. I don't personally want to be on the other end when he hears we've got Kohler triplets. I'll text you the address," he added. "See you shortly."

DeNucci had spent the night as the filling in a cat burrito. Her three felines had snuggled up against her and stared at her as if moving wasn't in their immediate plans. Gingerly, she squirmed toward the headboard, pulled her legs out and stumbled to the bathroom without disturbing them. The clock read 5:30 a.m.

As agile as an obstetrician who comes to life and speed-dresses in seconds when charge nurses call, the detective threw on the workout pants and a hoodie she hung on the back of the door for such occasions. She stopped to fill the cat's food bowls before darting out. Her only pit stop was at the first drive-in she spotted. She ordered two large coffees.

She'd grab a bite later. Bloated bodies, she recalled from her first water-related homicide, had taught her a hard lesson about her stomach's reaction to 'body-blimps.' She had left her bagel on the dock that night and never again brought breakfast to a drowning.

Bathtubs, DeNucci decided upon encountering this body, did an equally thorough job of pumping up a body to twice its size. Though interred within the confines of the oversized spa tub for more than a few hours, the infamous, now-retired hotelier (also known as Hell-telier Eve Shapiro) was still easy to identify. She looked like Shapiro on steroids.

DeNucci handed a paper cup of coffee to a grateful Archer as she took in the room. Forensics would think they'd gone to heaven when they saw the room they had to work in once more, but she was betting they'd come up as empty as they did at the others.

"Side benefit of plastic surgery over-kill," DeNucci told Archer. "I'll bet her face would be twice its size if it hadn't been stretched like a leather drum." She studied the body for a moment, realizing floaters always looked like oversized parade balloons. She backed up a step to check out the floor area abutting the tub and glimpsed something metallic peeking from the loopy weave of the white bathmat.

It turned out to be a key.

"Well, I'm ready to plan a party," she said sarcastically, picking it up. "It's been three days and this is the first time

I've actually found something out-of-place," she marveled. "I think God said, 'Enough! Christina showed up for all of her catechism classes back in the day—I'm gonna cut her a break today.'"

"God said that...?" Archer mimicked.

"He did. I take it you don't get any up close and personal messages from Him," she added, walking to the front door. It slipped into the latch. Perfect fit. "Be still my heart," she said to nobody in particular. "Archer," she yelled, "soon as someone gets here, have them run this to the lab ASAP."

The elegant town home revealed just about as many secrets as the Caron and Salazar sites. Big money spent on furnishings. Rows of photos, none of which looked family-friendly. Pristine surfaces, carpets, floors and appliances. Hospitals could take a lesson from these places, DeNucci remarked when criminalists reported they had found nothing.

Uncharacteristically losing patience, DeNucci spent hours pulling out drawers and collecting shreds of evidence, but as usual, there was nothing out of place. She was so focused, the ring of her cell phone made her jump. The news, however, couldn't have been more welcome.

There were fingerprints on the key. Jessup reported the lab had found a match to someone in the system. She urged the detective to get back to the precinct, promising to find the suspect and have them waiting. With the body "strained" and bagged and the lab techs done, she was out of there.

"Yup," DeNucci said to Archer as she darted by him, "God is on the job."

5—Families That Pray Together, Stay Together

As promised, Sarah Jessup had the suspect in the Shapiro murder sequestered in an interrogation room. Jessup didn't say a word. She pointed DeNucci toward a one-way mirror that revealed a cement-block bunker. It was painted a shade of green that was so awful, squad members joked that perps confessed just to get out.

Her eyes traveled to the woman sitting at a table. She hardly looked like someone capable of taking out three people in four days. Possibly 50 years old. Obviously Hispanic. She didn't look like someone who traveled in Caron or Shapiro circles.

Hang Salazar on a showerhead? Not likely. Only Shapiro could have been a victim at this woman's hands and when she perused the paperwork on the door she was about to enter, she felt her heart leap with excitement.

"Mrs. Anna Maria Gonzalez?" she asked, entering the room. "I'm Detective Christina DeNucci. It says here that you clean Mrs. Shapiro's townhouse."

The woman wore a deer-in-the-headlights look that became even more expressive when the detective spoke to her.

"Si, I clean up her house every day," she answered.

"You live in? I didn't see a maid's quarters."

"No. I go to Senora Shapiro every day on the bus. She no let anyone live there."

"So, you have a key to the place?"

"Si, I had a key. It got lost."

"Lost."

"Go missing," the maid clarified.

"I get it," the detective answered. "When were you there last?"

"Wednesday. I clean the house while Mrs. Shapiro work at home and then I leave. I not go back because she no give me all of my money. She say I eat too much of her food." The maid ended the sentence with a haughty neck snap.

"She cut your pay 'cause you ate her food?"

"She is very—how you say—firm with her money."

"Firm? You mean tight?"

"That, too. She look in the refrigerator after I come and when I go home."

"Let me cut to the chase here—where were you yesterday morning?" The detective had written a couple of notes, then flipped over the page anticipating the information.

"At Maids Manana. I register with them. When Mrs. Shapiro let me go, I go back to the agency for new assignment. I was there." She sniffed the air and held tightly to the large, well-worn purse that took up her entire lap.

"We retrieved a key from the bathroom—it was beside the tub where we found Mrs. Shapiro's body. Any idea how it got there?"

"My key?"

"What do you think? Your fingerprints are on it. That's how we found you. Immigration records. You were fingerprinted when you got your green card."

"Could be my key. I don't know. There are many houses to clean in this city. Many keys to hold. I stay with Mrs. Shapiro because I have patience. I raise 13 children," she explained with pride.

The detective lifted an eyebrow and looked her over. "13 children."

"Si. I have much patience. This is why I be sent to Mrs. Shapiro's. Lourdes could not work for her."

"Lourdes?"

"Si. Lourdes Gonzales. My sister-in-law."

The detective stopped writing. "Did your sister-in-law work for Giselle Caron?"

"Mrs. Caron, she is dead."

"Yes, she is. I don't mean to be rude, but don't you think it's a little coincidental that both of you have bosses that died within the last few days?"

"Si. But, it's tres," she held up three fingers.

"Three dead bosses?"

"Si. I have another sister-in-law."

The detective looked up again, "I don't suppose she worked for a guy named Salazar."

"She did. He's dead, you know."

"Yeah, I know. What's her name?" The detective's mind was racing.

"Susannah. Susannah Gonzalez. She work for Mr. Salazar."

"I'm going to hate myself for asking this question, but stay with me. How many sisters-in-law do you have?" She had put down her pad and was leaning against the table staring straight into Anna Maria's face.

"Six."

"Jesus Christ," she said in a tone so loud it scared the maid. Anna Maria pulled back from the table clutching her purse tighter.

"Okay. I need all of their names right now and contact information."

Anna Maria opened her purse. She placed crackers, wads of used tissue, a wallet, tin of aspirin, headscarf and more on the table before locating a beat-up address book. She turned to the "G's" and read, Lourdes, Susannah, Fatima, Marisol, Carolina and Bridget.

"Bridget?"

"Si. One brother, he don't like Latinas."

The detective picked up the intercom and called for Archer. It took a few minutes before he poked his head into the interrogation room. "Archer, I need you to round up these six ladies immediately."

He looked at the list and stopped. "Isn't this the woman who dropped her Hoover® on my foot?" he asked.

DeNucci rolled her eyes. "Just find these women," she said.

He started closing the door, but swung it open again. "Bridget?"

She ignored his question. "Archer, please have someone call Maids Manana and see if these ladies are registered. We may have four more surprises awaiting us if we don't move fast—and frankly, I'm not sure I'm ready to see how creative this group can get."

6—Flushed with Success

While she waited for the round up, DeNucci went to the ladies room to gather her thoughts. The room had been added to the precinct building after-the-fact—after women were more actively recruited and the need for separate facilities proved critical. She looked around the white expanse and checked out the appliances, scratching her head. Sarah Jessup came out of one of the stalls.

DeNucci's hands were on her hips. "So we've got the shower and tub accounted for and the plunger covers the toilet. What in God's name do you think could be left to use as a weapon?"

"Shower brush down the throat," Sarah said seriously. "Drano® in the eyes and mouth."

She shook her head. "Sarah, this is just so wrong. It's wrong."

"Razor to the throat," Jessup continued. "If the person's short, you could shove them into the sink faucet and impale them on it. Rip off the glass mirror and make a nice shiv."

The detective put up a hand to silence her. "Okay, okay. Let's stop thinking of methods and go to motive. Why would a bunch of maids start killing their clients?"

"Blackmail? Maybe one of them tried and the boss threatened deportation. With the exception of Bridget, of course," Sarah said.

"How did you know about Bridget?"

"You joking? It's all around the precinct." She took a bag of M&Ms® out of her pocket, offered some to DeNucci, and then spilled some into her hand.

"You eat in the bathroom?" DeNucci asked incredulously.

"It's gonna end up here anyway. I can eat anywhere," Sarah confided.

"What about floaters?"

"Are we talking water-logged bodies or bowel movements?"

"That's it. We're out of here," DeNucci said, throwing up her hands as she left the room.

It had taken hours to round up what everyone had begun calling the Gonzalez Gang. By late afternoon, seven domestics gathered round the table in the green interrogation room. The noise level, as they chatted among themselves in English, Spanish and Spanglish, was impressive.

Word of the roundup had spread quickly. A steady stream of visitors peered into the chamber to observe the group's lively banter. On the table around which they gathered, someone had dumped what appeared to be a purge of break room vending machines. Chip and pretzel bags, candy bar wrappers and plastic bottles of soft drinks littered the table. It had kept the group from mutinying until all seven were accounted for.

"Please put these on," DeNucci instructed the group as she entered and placed a sheet of nametags on the one spot devoid of food and beverage containers. Each woman's name had been lettered onto a tag. She could only pick out Lourdes, Anna Maria and Bridget, so she let each woman choose their tag.

The thought that they might switch nametags for whatever diabolical reason entered DeNucci's mind, so she made a copy of each woman's photo-embellished document card. Archer would be responsible for double-checks. Once he confirmed the matches, she switched on the video camera set up in the corner of the room and began.

"For those of you who don't know me, I'm Lieutenant Christina DeNucci and you're here because we want to ask you some questions about three murders that have taken place over the last few days. Does anyone here need a translator?" she asked. A collective, indignant "No, no" resounded from the group.

It took just a moment for DeNucci to realize that she wouldn't have language barrier issues. If anything, a bilingual stenographer might be required to draw up statements. As quickly as the questions began to fly, back came ready—if not proud—admissions of guilt from each of the women.

"The Senora Caron—she's a pig." Lourdes spit the words out as DeNucci held up her hands and silenced her in mid-sentence. Mindful of the cases lost at trial because statements were given before suspects could be given their rights, she Mirandized the entire group, asked again if a translator was needed and resumed the questioning.

"Senora Caron—complain, complain, complain. The bathroom, it's not clean enough, never clean enough. I see Joan Crawford movie. She like that. Only no hangers." Lourdes continued, a pressure cooker grateful for the chance to blow off steam.

"She drag me into the bathroom by my apron and make me plunge the toilet, then I have to use bleach to clean it while she watch. I have enough. I wait until Senora go into the bathroom to shower for work and I pin her to the floor. I use the plunger. Is very clean."

"Did the rest of you know she was going to do this?" DeNucci asked.

"No, but we like the idea," Carolina volunteered. "These people are rich and stupid and, como say llama—mean. They are mean."

"And Roberto Salazar?" DeNucci asked.

Susannah raised her hand. "I get help," she responded. "I am feeling good after Lourdes takes out her boss. I see on "Law & Order" how many people make a murder together. I could not have hung up Senor Salazar by myself," she explained.

The others nodded in agreement. "He was very slippery," she added. "Four of us get into the shower. Lucky I have a clothesline in my purse. We put the rope around him and tie it to the bar. He beg. We no care. We get very wet, but we clean up."

"Who helped?" DeNucci asked.

Lourdes, Anna Maria and Carolina raised hands in the air.

"Fatima, Marisol and Bridget," The detective asked, addressing the others, "Did you help Anna Maria kill Mrs. Shapiro?"

"Si," the three said enthusiastically and in unison, as though finally winning admission to an exclusive club to which they had been denied entry for decades.

"We no want to be left out," Marisol said proudly. "We want to be "Law & Order" ladies, too."

The crowd erupted in a barrage of chatter. Fingers were pointed as each of the women attempted to explain the various offenses that had reigned down on them from their super-rich employers.

Frankly, the tales were telling and DeNucci could understand why this group of domestic workers became enraged enough to plot their employer's murders. From Shapiro's monitoring of food consumption to Salazar's insistence that each tile in the bathroom had to be hand-scrubbed daily with a toothbrush were beyond excessive, pushing the women to the brink of collective indignity.

Christina had a flash of what Giselle Caron must have

looked like waving that plunger in the air while criticizing her maid's ability to maintain the toilet to this arrogant woman's standard. Hell, she thought, I'd be ready to take these folks out myself.

Of course, economic circumstances left each in a powerless position. Only the group's collective patience kept the women from strangling their demeaning bosses, and when Lourdes' morning encounter with Giselle Caron and the plunger pushed her over the edge, and once started, the spree gathered momentum.

DeNucci had never in her career felt so many conflicting emotions. She contacted a legal aid society established to represent immigrants with no money and explained their story. When they had been searched, photographed and booked, she helped shepherd them to vans. They would be transported to the women's jail where they would remain until arraigned by the court.

She couldn't help but have a bit of respect for what they had done, though she kept her thoughts to herself.

They say complete power corrupts completely, DeNucci thought, and in the case of the Gonzalez Gang, a bunch of women who had been pushed into submission one time too many decided to risk it all to take back some dignity. Gutsy, she thought.

"It's hard to dislike them," the detective said from her bar stool at the Sixty-Ninth Precinct. Jessup nodded in agreement, lifting her shot glass and proposing a toast to the Gonzalez Seven. Joey Archer had joined them. He still had a slight limp from where Lourdes Gonzales had come down on his foot with her industrial-size vacuum, but bore no grudge.

"I think I'll have a Margarita, no salt," he said to the bartender. "A little tribute to the ladies who said 'no more' to the jerks who used them like—well, toilet paper."

"Speaking of toilet paper, could someone tell me who decorated my car this week?" DeNucci asked, glaring at both of them.

"Don't look at me," they said in unison.

"Great. I guess this goes to Cold Case," she responded with a smile.

The trio swiveled on their stools to follow a gorgeous woman exiting the rest room. They nodded in agreement as they watched her leave the bar exuding dignity and grace. She opened the bar's door and a light breeze caught her skirt—and something below it.

None of them, they silently agreed, would go after her to tell her that a fluttering ribbon of toilet paper was stuck to her shoe.

Section Four: Sink or Swim

From the Desk of Mr. Man-ners

Dear Mr. Man-ners:

My husband is a slob. Since we share a bathroom I insist that it be kept to the highest standards. Towels should be folded and placed on the towel rack with monograms facing outward, the toothpaste should always be capped when not in use, hair products, skin care items and the like should be kept in plastic containers and neatly stored under the sink, the toilet seat should be wiped down after each use and the shower tiles need to be squeegeed and dried after each shower. BUT, Mr. Manners, this is not happening. Towels are balled up and tossed in the corner, his products are all over the place and the toothpaste...well I can't even go on. Please write back and talk some sense into my husband. You're the only hope I have left.

Desperate

Dear Desperate:

Mono-grams is ONE word (monograms). So is couple—and there is no I in couple! You married your husband for better or for worse. Get used to the worst since most people live into their 70's nowadays. Another option is to get a maid. To gain your husband's approval on this issue I suggest you make sure the maid is under 30 and reports to work wearing a black outfit that accentuates her bodacious bodice and lanky legs. "Having" a French maid is every married man's wet dream. However, you are not.

Mr. Man-ners

The Bath

by Jennifer Djordjevic

Cold cracked tiles
The familiar weight of feet
Belonging to a soul in pain
The tub waits patiently as she climbs in
Water scalds, washes away the filth of her wrongdoings
But still she hurts
Silver winks with each flick
A red ribbon its reward
Soon the water no longer burns as her pain dissolves
Turning her world a carefree pink

When It Rains...

by William D. Hicks

Water pounding against Jon's skin always made him feel as if he were floating above himself, almost as if he were astral projecting back in time along his own historical lifeline. This was when Jon remembered his own past with a vibrancy and realism that gave him true clarity, like now.

Hard droplets fell on his head like torrential sheets of rain during a hurricane. He turned toward the water and let it beat on his face. It felt wonderful; hot and steamy, hard and good.

Jon remembered when he'd started coming here. He was just 12 years old. Like most boys he'd been interested in his own body, but the only place he could explore what was solely his and no one else's, had been behind a locked door. Since his bedroom didn't have a lock, he had to go into the one bathroom in the house to read the smutty magazines he'd found in the garbage behind the neighborhood firehouse.

"Jonathan Schneider!" His foster mother banged on the

door again. It was the third time. "There are other people in this house who need to use the washroom. Get your ass out here now! Otherwise, I'm giving you back to the social worker. Do you want that?"

Jon used to fear these types of threats. Worrying that being placed in a different foster home would make it more and more difficult for his mother to find him. But he quickly realized foster parents would never give up the income they received from the state because of something as minor as hogging the bathroom. So, Jon had no intention of getting out of the bathroom. This was the only place he could learn what he needed to know—behind this locked door.

Besides that, his foster mother worked third shift at the diner, so she would have to leave soon to make it on time. Then she would go out for drinks, and return drunk sometime the next morning—waking half the house as she stumbled through the door. This happened every night; it was the only constant Jon could count on in this house.

The five other foster kids weren't like real brothers or sisters. It wasn't anything like one of those after-school TV specials popular during the '70's, where the kids bonded into some close-knit family structure. In fact, he and the "fosters" he lived with all seemed focused on surviving the experience until they could move out on their own.

Even after escaping the foster system, life wasn't what he dreamed it would be; at least not so far. That was for sure. No wealth, no fame by the time he turned 19. No, that was not to be. Jon had always dreamed about these things. He'd even planned on them.

But that was a long, long time ago. It seemed like eons to Jon. In reality, it was nearly a decade. Jon was glad to be rid of his past baggage. Baggage that included three temporary families that fostered him to the tune of $200 per month from the state—most of which was spent on dope or drink or food, or some combination of the three. Never just food. And never to Jon's benefit.

He considered the inevitability of his future as hot shower droplets pelted his face and his chest. Jon enjoyed this. It felt like what making love in an African rainforest might feel like. Sometimes, Jon imagined the pounding was more like something, or someone, punishing him.

God was punishing him, wasn't He? Jon had no great skills. He had no great talent. He had no great wealth. He had no great looks. Still, he felt he deserved more. He wanted more. He had been born into the wrong family. He deserved the hot pelting water that felt like sulfuric acid melting skin off his worthless bones.

It was karma of some kind, Jon thought, as he let the now-almost-scalding water reach his nether regions. There could be no doubt. He was either being punished for something he'd done in a past life or something he'd done in this life. Jon knew it was true. It had to be. He always figured out the mysteries of life in here, in the shower, under the beating, pounding, intensely hot water.

"Jon, get your ass out of there." The familiar words floated over the hard spraying shower. This time it wasn't the voice of a foster parent, but his girlfriend and roommate, Veronica Halstead.

"Sorry, Veronica. I didn't mean to hog the hot water." Jon dried his hair with the one towel he owned—a heavy pale-yellow Egyptian cotton one that looked as if it might have once been a bright vibrant sunflower color, but had lightened significantly before Jon bought it at the Salvation Army Secondhand Shop. He used the prized towel to quickly dry the rest of his body.

"Nice things deserve to be treated nicely," Jon said to nobody in particular. He folded the towel neatly over the towel bar above the toilet. This was where his towel went. He couldn't help loving the idea of owning this once-expensive towel, even though it now looked to some like a dirty rag. Someday, he would be able to afford his own brand-ass-new Egyptian cotton towels. Hell, someday maybe he'd even go to Egypt to buy them.

The door rattled in its frame. "Jon, Jon, Jon. I'm going to bust in on you—no matter what you're friggin' doing in there—I swear!" Veronica said.

Jon recognized this as a reenactment of a scene from a gangster movie they had watched together. He laughed. "Done," he said, flinging the door open dramatically, then walking naked past Veronica into their bedroom.

*   *   *

Black metal. White face. Red hands.

Jon stared at the clock. Ten minutes until he could leave. The end of his shift could not come soon enough. Then, Jon could take yet another shower and wash off the smell of bad Mexican food from his body and hair.

Art Landow, his best and only Taco Bell friend, sauntered up to him. "Hey man, I got the quick picks."

"Was it on the dollar menu?" Jon joked.

"No, the two dollar menu," Art replied.

They both laughed.

They'd been buying two lottery tickets since they began working together, some two years before. It was one of the few extravagances Jon could afford—even though his girlfriend Veronica complained that it was "like throwing two dollars into a wishing well and expecting a return on your investment."

Gary Ackerson, whose father owned this Taco Bell franchise, gave Jon and Art a suspicious look of disapproval. "Get back to work."

"I'm almost done for the day," Jon said, his voice thick with sarcasm.

"And you?" Gary pointed at Art.

"I'm on in five minutes," Art said. Then he walked hurriedly into the back of the restaurant.

Jon never understood how one of the hardest jobs in the world, fast food work, paid the worst wages. He had to be charming to soccer moms who insisted their children should be able to "explore" their world by touching and terrorizing everything, including the napkin and soda dispensers and making "artistic statements" with ketchup.

He had to refuse coffee to bums who claimed they wanted free refills in cups that were obviously days old, as evidenced by dumpster stains of everything one could imagine on the cup's surface. He had to clean up bathroom disasters that would terrify a trained triage nurse. To top it off, he had to deal with bosses like Gary Ackerson who thought "screw you" was a management style.

Jon had to do all this for $7.50 an hour with no bonuses and no days off. Well, to be honest, he could take days off; he just couldn't get paid for them. Not like office workers.

Then again, Jon couldn't get an office job with a high school diploma. While his grades hadn't been too bad, they hadn't been phenomenal either. So he knew he wasn't going to get some great scholarship. His only option, once he had moved out of his last foster home, was to get his first job at McDonald's. Still, it wasn't enough for a decent apartment. "Isn't it ironic?" Jon sometimes sang in the shower, quoting his favorite Alanis Morissette song, while droplets of hot water pelted his skin.

Eventually, Jon had found a better paying job at Taco Bell. Here he could "think outside the bun"—as their recruitment advertisement suggested. This was where he met, and eventually moved in with, his girlfriend, Veronica.

One minute left. The taco-shaped clock ticked off the

last remaining seconds. These torturous last moments felt like the minutes that ran into hours that ran into days when Jon hoped beyond all hope that his mother would rescue him from the hell that was his foster life.

The stink of beans which had been refried and refried and refried one more time almost made Jon gag. He wished he were home washing up right now. He could just imagine the hot, tingly hard water against his...

A heavyset, red-headed woman with about 15 Cub Scouts entered the restaurant just at that moment. She walked directly up to Jon.

Damn. Now he had to stay. It was a rule, a stupid rule, but one he had agreed to when he'd first signed on: If you had a customer, you had to take care of them, no matter when they arrived.

"Welcome to Taco Bell, may I take your order?" he droned.

"I know you don't really want to take my order."

"No...I'm..." Jon stammered.

"You're wishing I hadn't brought in Scout Pack 290. Boys, give this guy a big growl."

"Rowwwwr," the Cub Scouts responded, disinterestedly.

"Ma'am what can I get for you and Pack 290?" Jon said, trying to compose himself.

"Just because I'm older than you doesn't mean you can call me ma'am. I'm not that old."

Jon didn't know what to say. Obviously he was making matters worse. He was just trying to be polite and respectful. Plus, she was a lot older than he was.

His lack of instantaneous response must have irked the woman. "What you can get me is the manager. I want to register a complaint."

Jon wasn't sure what happened next. He tried to explain to Gary, his manager, what had transpired, but he didn't seem to care. That meant Jon was out.

Out of work and out of luck.

*   *   *

"But Jon, you know that's not the only time Gary called you on the carpet," Veronica said, "Remember, there was the time..."

Jon didn't hear which time Veronica was referring to. Of course he knew there had been other times. On occasion, he'd been reprimanded for saying the wrong thing to a customer. There also had been times he'd been unable to hold his tongue with the staff.

But this last time wasn't the worst, so Jon hadn't expected it to be the final straw.

"Don't you agree?" Veronica folded her arms over her chest and awaited an answer. An answer to what, Jon wasn't quite sure. Obviously she'd asked a question.

"Maybe." He couldn't answer yes or no. Maybe was the only thing that seemed safe.

"Did you even hear what the question was?"

Jon realized that "maybe" was never a safe answer. "No. But I'm sure you're going to tell me."

They were arguing again. Recently, that seemed like all

he and Veronica did. Was it always this hard when you loved someone? Jon wasn't sure since Veronica was the only woman he'd ever felt that strongly about. Usually, they argued about money or, more precisely, Jon's lack thereof. But today it was all about Jon's lack of a job or as Jon liked to think about it: What Jon did on his summer vacation after he lost his job.

"I asked you who was to blame for this happening."

"It wasn't my fault," Jon said, knowing what was coming next.

"I was hoping beyond hope you wouldn't say that. Jon, at some point, you have to take some responsibility for your life. Whose fault was it, the man on the moon? Maybe it was one of those foster parents you blame for everything."

"I don't want to talk about this Veronica. I just need a few days off. Then I'll go in and get unemployment. Then I'll have some money."

"That's not enough to live on Jon. Whose fault was it anyhow? And I don't want to hear how it was your mother's fault for abandoning you. You've used her as an excuse far too long."

"What? My mother was a bitch. She never came back for me. I lived in foster hell my entire childhood. Can't we just skip this argument and jump to where we're taking a shower together?"

"That's your solution to everything, Jon. Have you ever thought that maybe showering is just a substitute for your mother's womb?"

"I refuse to talk about this. I'll even move to the part where I'm giving you a massage after we've made love."

"Water and the womb. It makes sense. It explains every..."

"It explains nothing. Unless we're talking about your womb. You're worried about the fact that we won't be able to get married soon enough to suit your master plan."

"Jon, at least I have a plan. Haven't you ever had a plan? I want to be married by the time I'm 25. That's only a year away. At this rate, it will never happen for us. How can you expect to be able to support me—let alone a child? Yes, I want a child. I thought you did too. Maybe I am worried about my biological clock, but that's only because I want more from my life than just being a mother. I want a life after childbirth."

"I'm surprised you haven't penned in the exact date to remove your stretch marks." Jon hated himself for saying it, but he was frustrated, too. Sure he wanted those things. Of course Veronica was right. At this rate he, she, they would never have them. "I didn't mean..."

"I can't," Veronica said, holding out her hand to stop him. "Jon, I can't do this anymore." Tears rolled down her cheeks, smearing her meticulously applied makeup. "I'm leaving."

"I'm sorry. I didn't mean it. I'm frustrated..."

"No, I'm sorry; I just can't do this anymore."

"Okay, will you be at Jane's house?" Jane was Veronica's best friend, the woman she turned to in crisis.

Jon hoped some time away from each other would allow them both to cool down. "If that's where you'll be, I'll call you..."

"Please don't. I...I...think," Veronica said, dabbing at the tracks her tears made with a tissue she retrieved from her purse, "we need...I need...for us to be over. I'll have my brother help me move my things tomorrow. Try not to be here." She got up off the sofa, straightened her skirt and walked out of their apartment, allowing the front door to slam shut behind her.

*   *   *

"I'm sorry, but the Taco Bell manager said they fired you for cause."

"What cause? I didn't do anything," Jon told the clerk at the unemployment office. "It wasn't my fault." Jon flashed back to his fight with Veronica.

"...disrespectful to a customer. Calling her old. Arguing with the manager. He had an entire list."

"I never..."

"I'm sorry, if you'd like, you can write a letter explaining what happened and you'll be eligible for a hearing to reverse the decision."

"Will that fix everything? I can write it right here. I need the money. I know it's not a lot, but I need to pay..."

"Sir. You can write the letter at home and mail it into us. Then we will consider awarding the benefits. But I can't promise anything. Now, if you will please leave my office, I have other people I need to help."

Jon left the unemployment office devastated. Even the thought of being able to go home and take a soothing shower that could last off-and-on half the day, didn't make him feel any better. He'd been out of work for a week. He'd never been out of work before so he thought he'd take a break. Eventually, he'd come into the unemployment office. He'd been certain they would give him the benefits. After all, he hadn't done anything wrong.

On the bus, Jon replayed all that happened to him in the previous month. It played like a bad movie in his mind. The red-haired woman's attitude. Scout Pack 290, "Rowwwwr." Gary, the Taco Bell manager, firing him. Veronica's constant nagging. The breakup. Unemployment refusing to pay. Ghosts of his foster days. The love-hate he felt for his biological mother. Did he have anything left to hang onto?

Shower—it will make it better—his inner voice was telling him. Take a long shower. You'll figure it out in there, where you can daydream, where you can sort out what you need to do next.

Once again, Jon got that sense that he was being punished. That he'd done something wrong in his past or present life. For the past week he'd tried to figure out what it was. What had he done wrong? But now there was another feeling intermingled with that sense of being punished. It was a good feeling...relief. Could it be he was relieved to be gone from the world of fast food?

Of course he was, but it wasn't just relief he was feeling

as he made his way home on the bus—it was acceptance. While he was relieved that all his options—all those possibilities that once weighed so heavily on his mind were now gone—he also accepted that there was really only one option left that made any sense. The removal of choices made Jon experience a sense of calm he rarely felt in life.

Finally, the bus neared his home. The shower welcomed his arrival like a lover with open arms. Jon did a get-naked dance on his way from the front door to the bathroom. He was nude and under the water within two minutes of walking in the door.

The hot beating water felt wonderful on his skin. Relief washed over his psyche as water washed over his body. The shower provided Jon with one final moment of clarity, that of him as an unfulfilled man seeking things he could never have, and dying a lonely, bitter, old man who blamed other people for his failures.

This was a future Jon didn't want, though he knew this was how his life would probably end. All the things he once held dear would be gone. Perhaps his dreams were just that—dreams of a man who had never grown up. A man who blamed the world for not giving him what he felt entitled to; a life full of the finer things.

On top of that, the one truly good thing in Jon's life was gone; Veronica, the woman he had never expected to love. His life was in ruins. There was only one thing left to do.

Jon stepped out of the warmth of the shower. He

located the razor in the medicine cabinet. Quickly and with great agility he dislodged the blade. Then he stepped back into the shower, allowing it to embrace him with its warmth again.

No family. No job. No girlfriend. No life. No pain. Maybe a little pain, but only for a short time if he did it right.

Jon looked at the glistening blade as the clear water ran down its length. He moved his right hand swiftly to avoid thinking about what he was doing. He didn't want to become one of those pitiable souls who didn't have the nerve to make the ultimate life decision—when to end it.

He slashed his left wrist with the sharp edge of the razor. Then he moved the razor to his left hand and pressed as hard as he could on his right wrist. His wrists flared in pain as his blood mixed with the hot shower water. Soon the water turned pink and dripped down his hands and off his fingers to the shower floor below.

The blade slipped from Jon's grasp. He was floating again. Not in the past, but in the knowledge that soon he would have no future.

As he began to slip away he couldn't get the lyrics of the REM song "Everybody Hurts" out of his mind.

When you're sure you've had enough of this life...

"Jon! Jon!" Art bellowed from somewhere in the apartment. "Where are you man?"

...well hang on.

A long silence followed.

"Hey, I hear the water down the hallway," a female voice said.

Jon knew he was hallucinating. The voice sounded like...

There was a loud rapping at the bathroom door.

If you feel like letting go, (hold on).

"Jon, I know how you love your showers. But you've got to come out here right now," Veronica said in a playful, scolding voice. "You won't believe it," she said, gushing. "I couldn't either."

"Hey man, I had to stop and get Veronica. I know how bad off you've been since you two split. Everything's going to be okay now. We hit the lottery! Jon, we won. All we've got to do is..."

Water poured over Jon's skin. His wrists were on fire. His body felt heavy. His mind was fogging over. He was being punished. He couldn't have heard right. He wasn't a winner. He was a loser. His mother had known it. Even Veronica knew it. She'd as much as said it when she dumped him. This was all some kind of lucid death-dream. Or maybe his brain was doing some kind of death-hiccup.

Someone knocked again. It sounded sharper. More urgent.

Maybe...maybe, his mind thought...maybe it was real.

If you feel like you're alone, no, no, no, you are not alone.

Had he locked the bathroom door or not? Jon couldn't remember. He tried to hold on. Tried to stave off unconsciousness. He was losing. Death was winning. His body began to slowly sink into the shower floor.

"Something's wrong!" Veronica screamed.

"Calm down, Veronica," Art said. "Jon's just taking a long shower. You know he likes his showers hot and long."

"That shower's been on since before we arrived and we've been here awhile. The tank doesn't hold that much hot water. It must be frigid by now." Her voice cracked. "Jon detests cold water."

The shower droplets felt glacial. Normally, Jon knew this meant he'd exhausted the hot water supply. Right now it meant he was exhausting his last moments of life on Earth.

So, hold on, hold on, hold on, hold on, hold on, hold on, hold on, hold on.

Look Again
by Barbara Yohnka

I was so glad my shift had ended at the hospital. It had been a steamy August day and when it got that hot, tempers flared and the crime rate went up. There were several automobile accidents that evening, which meant that not only was the ER busy, but also the lab and x-ray departments. I barely had time to make a pit stop in the bathroom, let alone eat supper in the cafeteria, like I usually did every night with my boyfriend, John, a doctor in the ER.

The x-ray viewing area was overrun with residents and interns checking films, asking to schedule procedures, and wondering why the radiologist hadn't yet read their x-rays. I tried to explain that we were short-handed because of vacations. Nevertheless, they expected me to perform miracles; like call in radiologists, develop films like a kid on speed, and transcribe the reports. At any moment, I half expected someone to ask me to turn water into wine.

Wine. That sounded good. A whole bottle of wine. Beaujolais, a rich Burgundy, a Merlot, I didn't really care.

Wine was an excellent accompaniment for the Dracula movie I was watching that night after work. My friend Viki was picking up the DVD because she was off that day and all I had to do was go home, let out the dog, brush my teeth, pack my PJs and drive to her house. I ticked off the list as I drove home.

My Border Collie, Fig, knew the routine and while she did her business, I changed out of my scrubs to shorts, a tank top and sandals. Walking into the bathroom, I brushed my teeth and looked in the mirror, checking out my tan lines from the morning's tanning session. My cheeks looked rosy and freckled, but the stress of the day was reflected in my eyes. I hoped I could stay awake long enough to watch the movie.

I looked in the mirror again after rinsing my mouth and pulled my blond hair into a ponytail. Then I packed a nightshirt, snacks, and chocolate in my gym bag and whistled for Fig who came inside and waited patiently by the door for her treat.

"Sorry I have to leave you home tonight, Fig, but you and Viki's cats don't exactly get along," I said, petting her. "Don't worry; I'll be back home before you even wake up." She licked my hand before I locked the door behind me.

I was walking to my Sentra when I realized I'd forgotten to pick up the pictures my sister had emailed to Walgreen's. I'd planned to get them after work and get a frame for one of them for my desk but it completely slipped my mind. One more thing to add to tomorrow's growing list.

When I slipped my key into the car door I realized I hadn't locked it in my haste to get inside the house. I chastised myself because I was usually so particular about that.

Throwing my gym bag on the passenger seat, I fumbled around for my keys that I promptly dropped on the floor. Unexpectedly, the hair stood up on the back of my neck. I inhaled sharply and sat slowly back in my seat, glancing in the rear view mirror as I reached for my seatbelt, hoping my imagination was playing tricks with me.

No trick. There was a man behind me with a knife in his left hand. He pressed it against my neck, told me not to move, told me to shut my door.

"Start driving," he barked.

I put the key into the ignition. Actually I was praying the car wouldn't start but its recent tune-up made that unlikely. Putting the car into drive, I traveled up the street trying not to hyperventilate while the stranger pressed the knife sharply to my throat.

"Turn right," he said, his voice gravelly. I followed his directions.

I glanced again in the mirror and caught his gaze. "Why are you doing this? If you want money, you can have whatever I have in my purse. It's on the front seat."

"I don't want your fucking money. I got plans," he said, flashing a set of perfect teeth.

I drove for a few blocks and realized I'd be on a main thoroughfare in another block. He must have realized it as well.

"Turn left." He pressed the knife to my throat and leaning forward against the back of my seat. I could feel his breath on my neck.

"Go around the block and down towards the school." He was rubbing his finger behind my ear, pulling the hair out of its band. "Take your hair down. I like blondes with long, pretty hair."

Both hands were gripping the wheel so tightly that I didn't know if I'd be able to pry either loose.

"Now!" he yelled. I released my right hand and used it to slip the stretchy band out of my hair.

"You've got nice hair. Smells good too," he said running his fingers through it and down the nape of my neck. I was shivering from fright, despite the heat and his breath on my neck.

My hair, I realized, had distracted him, so I continued driving, seeing an opportunity to call attention to the car, possibly by driving up someone's front porch.

As if reading my mind, he said, "Don't fuckin' think about doing anything stupid. I got the whole night planned out. Turn right, then go two blocks and we'll be at the school."

I looked at him again in the mirror and saw deep brown irises surrounded by ultra white sclera, the protective area around the eye. Helluva time to remember my anatomy lesson, I thought.

"Like what you see?" He laughed, like it was the funniest thing he'd ever said.

"Not really." My mouth engaged before my intellect had a chance to respond. "You're not really my type."

"You got a type, huh? Like that tall boyfriend of yours? I seen him go to your house and leave in the morning. I'm getting me a piece of *his* ass."

He poked the tip of the knife at the tender area behind my left ear. I yelped in pain. By this time I realized a number of things—all of them flooding my brain at once. He'd been watching me. He probably was going to kill me. If he wasn't planning to kill me, why the knife?

In between thoughts about the stranger, my mind flashed pictures of my family and friends with subtitles like in foreign films. I'd never see my little niece again, never see my family, never find out if John was serious about moving in together, wouldn't even be able to pick up my paycheck. And damn! I had an anatomy and physiology test on Thursday. Dr. Katz didn't allow makeups. Shit! What could I do? Maybe if I played along and did what he told me, I'd be okay. I could get through it. I could...

"Turn in here." He switched the knife into his right hand. "Pull up right alongside the building."

"I don't think I can fit my car through there," I said, my voice tremulous.

"You're not here to think. Get the fuck outta' the car!" The next thing I knew he was standing outside opening my door. "See what a gentleman I can be?"

He put his right arm around my neck and moved the

knife to his left. He walked closely behind me so he could lead me where he wanted me to go. I tried to check out my surroundings, glimpsing a 12-foot tall chain link fence to my left and the side entrance to the school on my right. The ground was rough. Pitted areas filled with leaves and small branches had settled into the yard over a mix of gravel and asphalt, common to school-yards and parking lots. I imagined the grade schoolers playing hopscotch and hoped they were more coordinated than I was at their age. I was forever tripping over my own feet.

He walked me to the entrance that was sheltered by a stone roof and surrounded by an apron of cement with two stairs that led to the grated door. "Stop right there. We got us some privacy now."

He pushed me up against the door and the handle hit the small of my back. I tried to wriggle away but he pushed me harder. I hadn't looked at him full on but with his face mere inches from mine, his hands on my arms, his knee between my legs, I didn't have a choice.

He was a young man, dark complexioned—probably African-American, medium build, my height. I momentarily thought that if I used all my strength I might be able to push him away. I was working up the courage to do it, realizing I'd have to touch him when he yanked the strap of my tank top and bra down my right shoulder.

"Take this off." He nuzzled the underside of my jaw. "Take all your clothes off," he added as an afterthought.

Stalling, I reached behind me to unsnap my bra, hoping to forego getting totally naked.

He pushed against me again, this time using one hand to unbutton and unzip my shorts. If I were undressing myself, or undressing for John, I'd have shimmied out of them but I wasn't alone or with John and this was certainly no time for anything that might encourage the stranger.

I was standing in my flip-flops, with my shorts around my ankles, displaying my new black underwear for this creep and feigning having trouble removing my bra. He was having none of that. Grabbing the hem of my top, he pulled the shirt up over my head, ripped the bra away, and pushed me harder against the door.

"I'm tired a waitin', Bitch. Down on the ground."

Using the door for support, I tried to slide down easily so I wouldn't tumble, but having my shorts more off than on and now under the heels of my sandals, made gracefulness a task. He reached down and grabbed my shorts, folding them under his arm, and motioned for me to lie on the ground.

"Put these under your head," he ordered, handing the shorts to me.

At this angle, the moon provided a sliver of light in the darkened passageway, enough to illuminate my body as I tried to lie on the ground.

"You got nice tits." He unzipped his khaki pants.

I closed my eyes and the next thing I knew he had

reached roughly between my clenched legs and yanked off my underpants, forcing my knees apart. He knelt between my legs and lay on top of me. He tried to kiss me but I turned my head and uttered, "No."

"Have it your way, Bitch," he said. "Think about your boyfriend while I'm doin you and think about how good this is going to feel..." He grunted. "For me, that is."

I thought about my little niece who, according to her grandma, had evidently inherited the genetic sassiness so common among the females in my family. I would miss my mom. If he killed me, she'd never know how much I appreciated her. She'd only have the memories of our last disagreement.

"Oh my God, I am heartily sorry, for having offended Thee," I prayed, hoping he'd finish, get up and leave without hurting me further. Sitting up, he grabbed my legs and his face was filled with moonlight. I could see his wide smile, the red baseball cap turned backwards, revealing a shiny scalp over thick eyebrows. And those eyes. A perfect nose and full lips completed the mug shot I'd drawn in my mind.

"Get a good look so you can tell your boyfriend," he said putting the knife down to his left side. He grabbed my wrists together with his left hand and roughly ground my right breast with the right.

My eyes gravitated towards the knife, which was within my reach, if only he hadn't held onto my wrists so tightly. Again he seemed to read my mind and said, "Don't get any ideas. I'ma move this knife and let your hands go. Put your arms around me."

"No."

"I'm not playin'! Put your arms around me!"

Not seeing an alternative, I did as he said. He lay on top of me again and his movements speeded up. I heard grunts yet tried to block them out with a nursery rhyme I sang to my little niece when she was a baby. "Rock-a-bye, don't you cry, go to sleep little baby..."

My skin felt ultra sensitive and the seams from his pants grazed my legs and scraped my thighs as he...

Moments later, he stood up, zipped his fly, took off his cap, and bowed, saying, "It's been cool, Mama. I'll be seein' you around." He laughed then sprinted back down the passageway.

It took me a minute to assess my situation. I'd been raped but otherwise, he hadn't hurt me physically. I sat up, leaning on my elbows which made me whimper, as there was more gravel beneath me than I had previously noticed. I still had on my flip-flops but my shorts were behind me, their use as a pillow no longer necessary. My tank top and bra were about 10 feet away, wadded up like a ball. My underwear was caught on a nick on the concrete stair, and clung to it as if it naturally belonged there. So much for my Victoria's Secret splurge.

Leaning on my right arm, I pushed myself up, brushing off the gravel that clung to my sticky, sweaty skin. It had to still be over 90 degrees and it was midnight or later.

I turned around and picked up my shorts, stepping into them one leg at a time. I picked up the panties and shoved them in my pocket. I found the bra and tank top, untangled them and put on my bra, followed quickly by the shirt. I smoothed everything out, as if I were getting up from an unexpected nap and slowly walked towards my car. I'd presumed he'd really left and I was right.

The dome light was on in my car as he apparently had not shut the door all the way. I wondered if the neighbors heard anything, or noticed a car parked in this driveway of sorts. Perhaps they thought we were teenagers looking for a little private place. But they would've been wrong.

I walked to the car, checked out the back, and then sat in the driver's seat. Nothing was disturbed and my purse and gym bag were right there on the passenger's side where I left them. There was only one thing to do—call the police. I checked the back pocket of my purse and searched through lipstick tubes, breath mints, Nutrasweet™ packets, and pens but found no phone. I must've left it at home.

The keys were in the ignition and as I started the car, I looked in the mirror, half expecting the man to be looking back at me. It gave me the chills. I backed the car out and when I got to the street, made a U-turn and headed for the Main Street Police Station, ironically, only three blocks away.

Pulling into the station parking lot, I grabbed my purse, and locked the door as I nervously entered the reception area. There was a male officer sitting at a desk in the lobby. As I approached him I started to shake and realized I had to use the restroom.

"May I help you, Miss?"

"Yes, officer. I want to report a crime."

"What type of crime?"

"I've been raped."

"Let me get a female officer. Why don't you sit on the bench; she'll be here in a moment."

"May I use the restroom?"

"Yeah, it's down the hall and to your left."

"Could somebody go with me?"

"Sure. Officer Johnson will be right with you. You're welcome to stay right here until she comes downstairs."

There was a buzz of activity in the area to the right of the officer's desk. Two men in handcuffs, three police officers, and a woman and her child were all arguing. I moved from foot to foot until I saw a female officer walk up to the desk. She spoke to the first officer, turned around, and addressed me.

"Miss? I'm Officer Johnson. Let me take you to the ladies room," she said, gesturing for me to follow her.

The slap of my flip-flops on the marble floor made me feel self-conscious and I hurried to catch up with the officer. She unlocked the door, checked inside, and said, "I'll be right outside; don't worry. You're safe here."

I walked inside the restroom and faced myself in the mirror. My hair hung in clumps down my face and neck, looking nothing like the perky ponytail I had when I left home. But my eyes scared me. I looked closely into the mirror and saw fear there. I closed my eyes, counted to ten, and opened them again. The stranger was standing behind me, his arms crossed, a shit-eating grin on his face. I screamed.

Officer Johnson flew into the restroom, asking, "Are you okay? What happened?"

"He was here!"

"I'm sorry, Miss. No one came in."

"He must've been hiding in here," I said frantically.

"I checked all the stalls before I let you come in. No one was here. Look, I'll stay right here so you can use the toilet. It'll be okay. I promise," she said, trying to reassure me.

Tears flooded my eyes as I slowly walked to the first stall, clutching my purse to my chest. I pushed the door open before I entered and when I was sure I was alone, and the door was bolted, I dropped my shorts and urinated.

When I was finished, I unlocked the stall door and looked to my left, seeing Officer Johnson standing in front of the exterior door. I went to the sink and tried not to look at the mirror. I washed my hands then filled then with warm water to rinse off my face. Out of habit, I looked up and saw not only Officer Johnson, but also the stranger standing behind me.

"Go away!" I screamed and tears filled my eyes again.

Officer Johnson said, "Miss, we're the only two people

here. There's no one else in here." She grabbed some paper towels and handed them to me so I could dry my face. I couldn't stop crying.

"But I saw him," I whimpered. She told me we could go to her office and talk.

"Maybe he's outside. He could be hiding. He hid in my car. I didn't even know he was there. After he…raped me he virtually disappeared, he was gone so fast. How do you know he's not outside?"

"Miss, what's your name?"

"Liz, Liz Korie."

"Ms. Korie, this is a police station. We make sure that people who come to us for help, get help and we don't let anything happen to them while they're here. Would you like to come with me and we can talk? Then perhaps there's someone you can call, okay?"

I nodded and let Officer Johnson lead me to her office on the second floor. I walked beside her, looking behind me several times to make sure we weren't being followed. When we reached her office, she sat behind her desk. I sat across from her while she documented my answers to her questions and gave me some information on procedures for a sexual assault.

"As part of the protocol I have to take you to the hospital so they can do a rape kit. Are you willing to do that, Ms. Korie?"

"Yes, but you're going with me, right?"

"Of course, but isn't there someone you want to call?"

"I should probably call my friend, Viki. I was driving to her home when the, when this happened. She's probably wondering why I haven't showed up yet. I could also call my boyfriend, John. No, I'll just call Viki."

After Officer Johnson dialed the number, I spoke to my friend and assured her I would be all right. I told her that I was going to the hospital but that the policewoman was going to accompany me. With that I handed back the phone, gathered my purse, and proceeded to follow the officer outside to her car.

I was hesitant to leave the station but with Officer Johnson beside me, I walked to the lot and entered the squad car.

"What hospital are we going to?" I asked, as we drove down Main Street.

"St. Joseph's."

"We can't go there! I work there. People will find out. Why do we have to go there?" I yelled and started to cry again. "And John works there, too."

"John's your boyfriend."

"Yes!"

"It might be good that he's there. He can help you get a..."

"Why do you have to go there, to St. Joe's?"

"It's procedure, Ms. Korie. I'm sorry. The people who work there are bound by confidentiality. I promise you that no one will find out. You'll have a doctor examine you and a nurse will be there and I'll be right outside the door, waiting to take you home when you are finished," Johnson said.

I resigned myself to going to St. Joe's where I had spent five out of every seven days, for the past five years, on duty in the x-ray department; St. Joe's, where Dr. John Thomas, my boyfriend of two years worked; St. Joe's, where my face was a fixture and I knew practically everyone on staff, from administration to the newest custodian. Officer Johnson may think that no one will find out but I know St. Joe's and by tomorrow morning, everyone will know what happened to me.

Considering that St. Joseph's Hospital was only six blocks from the police station, we arrived at the emergency entrance in less than five minutes. I remained in the back seat of the cruiser until Officer Johnson opened the door for me. She walked with me through the automatic doors that led to ER reception, and went ahead of me to the check in window to tell the clerk that "the rape victim" was waiting to be seen by a doctor. I took a seat in the farthest corner of the waiting room and grabbed a magazine to hide behind.

A couple of minutes later, Officer Johnson, and a nurse, whom I knew, of course, walked me to an exam room. The nurse, whose name was Beth, whispered, "Liz, I'm so sorry. I had no idea it was you. Don't worry, we'll take good care of you and I'll be with you the whole time. Doctor will be in momentarily. I'll be right back with the kit," she said, as much to me as to Officer Johnson.

"Officer Johnson? You said no one would know," I said, trying to hold back my tears.

"That nurse is a professional. She's trained to handle these situations professionally. I still don't think you have to worry," she said, patting me on the arm.

"I just want this to be over."

"Once the doctor comes, I'll step outside and the nurse will assist him or her in going through the rape protocol. It really is a good thing that St. Joe's subscribes to this procedure; there are several hospitals in the area that don't," she said.

"Yeah. I'm just lucky all the way around."

As I waited, I sat on the edge of the exam table, my legs swaying back and forth like a two-year old kid on a swing. Every time I looked at the door, Officer Johnson smiled at me. I just wanted the doctor to arrive and to finish this exam.

I had just finished that thought when I heard the doorknob turn and in walked the physician—none other than Dr. John Thomas, my boyfriend.

"Liz! I had no idea, Honey!" he said, embracing me.

"No! I don't want you here! Don't touch me! Let me go!" I yelled and jumped off the table, ran out the door, and down the hall to the restroom.

Once inside I locked the door behind me. I stepped back until I was leaning on the vanity. Again, out of habit, I looked in the mirror. The rapist appeared behind me.

"You can't run away from me."

"You're not here! You're not real!"

I heard pounding on the door and John's voice. "Open the door, please. I want to help you. We can get someone else for the exam but I want to help you because I love you. Please come out," he pleaded.

The rapist smiled at me. "You think that's your boyfriend outside? It's not him. If you open the door, I'll still be there, lookin' at you, smilin' at you, remembering what we did together." He laughed.

"We didn't do anything together. You raped me."

"It didn't feel like rape to me. You seemed willing. You took off your clothes when I asked, didn't you?"

"I had no choice. I did not consent to having sex, that aberration you call sex."

John's voice returned. "Liz, I'm here with the officer. We just want to help. Let us help. Let me help."

"Don't open that door," the rapist said. "Your boyfriend's not there; the officer is not there; but I'm there and I'll be there every time you look in the mirror. Again and again."

I turned around to face the mirror. The rapist stood behind me. I could see him smiling while he moved closer to me and knew I had to fight back this time.

I saw the metal trashcan on the floor near my right foot. I looked in the mirror again. I saw the rapist smiling. I picked up the trashcan and flung it at the mirror with all the strength I possessed. The mirror shattered into a thousand pieces, and with it, went the image of the rapist.

Although I had shielded my eyes somewhat, I was still covered in tiny slivers. As I tried to shake them off, the door opened and Officer Johnson and John ran in.

"Are you okay, Ms. Korie?" Officer Johnson asked.

"I think I will be now."

The officer stepped into the restroom, took my arm, and walked me through the door.

Before I left, I looked towards the mirror again. I feared seeing the rapist's face leering at me but I only saw shards of glass.

"Oh God, Liz. I was so worried," John said, reaching out for me. When he took me in his arms, I realized that the next time I looked into the mirror, the rapist's face would only be a memory.

Water Flows

by William D. Hicks

Water flows like time in space...
From beginning to end...
Water flows like a swirling toilet...
Going round and round...
Water flows like a life lived...
Never slowing until the end.

He Grew Up

by *William D. Hicks*

A sanctuary
Of sorts.
Everything
Went wrong.
Out of sorts.
Mom and Dad
Lost the baby that
Was his brother.
Kids at school
Teased him
For crying
About what
He didn't know.
The bathroom
Was where
He went
A locked door.
Silence.
Peace.

Away
From people
From everything.
He could be
Someplace else.
With characters he dreamed
Of being.
In his books.
In his mind.
Away.
Eventually he stopped
Crying.
He wasn't sure why.
Eventually he grew up
He wasn't sure why.

White Snake

by William D. Hicks

Water swirled around me
like a bend in the Congo.
Up close,
It appeared
cloudy white.
That's why I didn't notice
the White Snake.
It came out of nowhere,
slowly,
slithering,
towards me,
as if to say
hello.
But this was not a social call.
I'd seen "Anaconda."
I was not stupid.
It shot out a white bar;
sure to be poison.
If it touched me

I would certainly die.
And yet the bar
was so large
it was impossible
to escape within
the confines
of my bathtub.
This was
not real.
I was not
a kid.
Not
anymore.
That bathroom.
This bathroom
Black granite countertop.
My head in the toilet.
The taste of Scotch.
Puking.
Too much alcohol.
Too much blow.
Too much fun.
Was this a flashback?
Or a flash forward?
I couldn't tell.
But I wondered this:
What if,
God forbid,

The poison
didn't need to touch me
to infect me?
The scariest
thought
of all:
Was the snake
a side effect
of the drugs
I'd consumed?
"What do you think?"
I asked no one.
Was the snake
A childhood dream
A fantasy
A rubber ducky of
My overactive
imagination?
Had I constructed it
to make
some semblance
of sense
out of my
all too unreal
life?
White. White. White.
"Inhale deeply."
"Feel the rush."

"Get high."
I'd heard them all.
Seduced
by too many drugs.
by friends who
were not friends.
Was this why
It was so simple
For the giant White Snake
to hypnotize me
into acquiescing?
Or was this the usual result
of yet another
three-day high?
I loved horror
as a kid.
In movies
In life.
Especially about
snakes.
Was this why
my life had turned
into something
so shocking
so absurdly
out of control?
A life half lived
is no life at all.

Hadn't slept
Hadn't eaten
—unless you count
the pills and coke
and alcohol.
Was this the present?
Or a fantasy gone wrong;
a horrid daydream
left over from last night
or twenty years before?
No matter.
It was a familiar,
drug-laced,
poison-induced
limbo.
A scene I'd lived before.
And I'd lived through them all.
Tonight,
the pain-reducing,
coma-inducing
specialty of the house
was my new favorite:
Coke with a Scotch chaser.
I grew mellow.
Lifted my head from the toilet.
Looked in the mirror.
A stomach devoid of food
for three days

would not be quelled.
Finished retching
and realized
I could not distinguish
the taste of past poisons
going in
From present poisons
coming out.
The mirror told the story.
White, it seemed,
was not my color.
Not on my nose.
Not on my face.
Not on my clothes.
A deathlike pale
enveloped my body.
Familiar. Awful.
White. White. White.
I wonder this:
If death had entertained me
Six months ago,
Would anyone I know
have noticed or cared?
Or am I dying,
in the mirror,
this very moment?
Is it possible
I just don't have

the good sense—
or energy—
to do as my broken spirit begs:
lie down
and be consumed
by the White Snake.

Section Five: The Outhouse Chronicles

From the Desk of Mr. Man-ners

Dear Mr. Man-ners:

After going out with a wonderful woman for two years, she is about to move in with me. There is only one problem: she has a cat. I don't hate the cat, but I hate the litter box and the fact that the cat's got to crap in the house. I can smell that thing rooms away. When I told my girlfriend I don't want the crap box in the kitchen, she says to put it in the bathroom. Frankly, I would rather not share my bathroom with another person all the time, much less with this feline. My girlfriend says, "Love me, love my cat." I don't know if I love her enough to love the cat and the crap box. What do I tell her?

Not Lovin' the Cat

Dear Not Lovin' the Cat

Two years and you didn't realize your girlfriend was attached to her...cat? How stupid are you? I say train the cat to use the toilet by itself. Though you may never get it to wipe—if you can train it to raise the seat after it pees, that's half the battle. Ask your girlfriend. She'll tell you I'm right. Your only other option is to break it off with your girlfriend by telling her you can't put up with the cat crap. Or, you could get a dog and let it use the house as it's personal backyard. She'll get the hint.

Mr. Man-ners

Grandma and Grandpa

by Jennifer Djordjevic

Gold shimmer
Pink shower curtain
Sparkles
Hairspray and hairnet
Razors and Old Spice
Heat lamps blazing hot pink
Safe
Soft worn towels
Curlers, bobby pins
Red lipstick, gold case
Bristle brush, thin comb
Cut-glass perfume bottles
White lace curtains
Glass block
Pink tile
Warm baths
Plastic lamp with colored lights

Just in Case

by Jim Szczepaniak

I had been warned in advance about the stick next to the toilet, and I prepared myself to deal with it— psychologically, and physically, if need be. I just wish someone had warned me about the pot.

This is a story about going back to a simpler, less antiseptic way of life. Also to a stinkier, sloppier one.

If you want to travel back to a time in America when people didn't take a shower every day, and didn't throw out scraps of food because it was wasteful, you have at least two options: you can enter the world of science fiction and take a trip to the past in a "way-back" machine. Or you can drive 93 miles due east from Chicago along Interstate 80/90 to South Bend, Indiana.

People in South Bend—at least the ones in my wife's family who still live there—do not shower daily. First, it's a waste of water. How clean do you really need to be? Second, they don't have a shower. They have a bathtub. There is one bathroom in the house. It's situated right alongside the kitchen and the dining room, with a door leading to each room. This proximity means that, when you have a house full of company, and someone needs to "do their business," as Aunt Lottie says, they have only steps to go from the kitchen, where everybody gathers at a family function, or the dining room, where everybody eats.

Although I am, by no means, a neat freak, I tend to be a bit squeamish when it comes to things in the bathroom department. For example, I do not think the best location for the only bathroom in a house is immediately adjacent to the kitchen and dining room. Some people make a lot of noises in the bathroom, even if they're not trying to, and some people make a lot of smells. I do not want to deal with either while I'm eating four feet away.

Given these foibles, I thank God my wife clued me in to some of the things I could expect before the first time we visited Aunt Lottie and Uncle Clem. Among those "things" is the wooden stick next to the toilet in the corner of the bathroom.

"You'll probably want to make sure you've done all your major daily bathroom duties before we go there," my wife explained. She shares her family's predilection for odd euphemisms for bodily functions.

When my wife was just a little girl, her mother told her, "Uncle Clem and Aunt Lottie have an old-fashioned house and something called a septic system. They save their money. They do not buy new things, like toilets that work properly. So when we visit them, there are some very special bathroom rules you'll have to follow. When you do your business, you can flush whatever comes out of you. But when you wipe yourself, you have to put the tissue into the wastebasket that sits next to the toilet. You can't flush the paper down because it will clog up the toilet and then the toilet will overflow and Mommy and Daddy will be very embarrassed and Uncle Clem will...well, just remember not to flush any paper down the toilet.

"There's a sign on the wall that will help you remember the rules. It reads, 'Just in case' and has an arrow pointing to the stick that leans against the wall. If you forget about the toilet tissue, hopefully you'll read the sign and that will remind you to use the stick to fish out the toilet paper and put it into the wastebasket before you flush.

"I know that's a lot to remember. So if you're in Aunt Lottie's bathroom and you forget how the rules work and get confused, just call for me. I'll be right outside the bathroom door, in the kitchen. Or outside the other door, in the dining room."

Needless to say, I had little desire to experience this South Bend lifestyle firsthand. But after years of invitations from Lottie and Clem, and years of excuses for why we couldn't make it, we decided to pay a visit. We took the trip along with my wife's sister, Diane (who was more than eight months pregnant) and her husband, Jack.

We were having a ferociously hot August, and we knew that the house did not have air conditioning. If these people wouldn't spend money on a toilet that flushed paper, they certainly weren't going to waste it on A/C. Before we started out, we called Aunt Lottie to ask if we could pick up fried chicken or something simple like that so she wouldn't have to cook on such a sweltering day.

"Oh, no," she said, hurt in her voice. "You're family! I have to cook. Especially for you. But I'll keep it simple."

As we listened to the radio on our drive to South Bend, the temperature kept going up: It was 96 when we left Chicago and 98 as we crossed the state line and 101 by the time we got to Clem and Lottie's. Stepping out of the air-conditioned car was like walking into a wall of heat while someone slapped a dripping wet bath towel over our heads.

I looked at my sister-in-law, her distended belly seemingly growing before my eyes. "If it gets too awful, just say you're not feeling well and we'll leave," I said in a fatherly, albeit conspiratorial, voice.

She sighed deeply and rolled her eyes. She looked drained. "I just need a big glass of ice water."

Before we could ring the doorbell of the old wood frame house, Lottie opened the door. Perspiration dripped off her skin, pasting the few wisps of grey hair trying to escape her tightly pulled-back bun against her wrinkled forehead. Her cotton housedress clung damply to her short but ample frame. A narrow patch of pasty pale leg showed above her knee-length support hose.

"Oh, thank goodness you're here!" she exclaimed. "The stuffed cabbage and beef roast have been ready for hours, but I've been keeping them in the oven so they don't get cold. We can sit right down to lunch. Come on in!"

In the two minutes since we'd gotten out of the cool car, my shirt was already beginning to drip, perhaps in sympathetic solidarity with Lottie's soaking shift. At least we'll be out of the sun, I thought, as I walked through the front door and was hit by a waft of air that felt hotter than the air outside. It also smelled sharp and sour.

"I think the sauerkraut might be ready, Lottie," said a raspy male voice from in the kitchen. "Who wants to give it a taste?"

Out from the kitchen came Clem, tall and slim, his thinning hair slicked back with Vitalis. He pointed a boney finger at Diane's stomach. "You're eating for two now! We'll make sure you get a lot of sauerkraut, so the baby learns to appreciate healthy food from the get-go!"

"Everyone take a seat around the dining table," said Lottie. "I'll just put out a stick of oleo for the rye bread and bring out the duck's blood soup. There's root beer and cream soda on the table. Would anybody like something else to drink?"

"I'd love a big glass of ice water," Diane said, wiping her sweaty forehead with the back of one hand.

"We'll get you some water," said Lottie, "but ice isn't good for anyone in this hot weather, especially for your baby." The corners of our hostess's mouth turned down disapprovingly. "You'll get sick. It's like going outside in cold weather with wet hair—you're just asking for trouble."

"Should we sit anywhere in particular?" I asked.

"Wherever you're comfortable," Lottie said. "Except the chair with the yellow polka-dot cushion over there. That's Clem's chair, on account of his hind-end issues. Oh, and I like to sit in the chair closest to the kitchen, so I can get up quick to bring food refills."

I scoped out the room layout. There, with the door ajar a few inches, was the bathroom. I decided to sit with my back to that door so I would not have to think about the just-in-case stick while Lottie piled course upon course on my plate.

"Diane, why don't you sit over there, next to the fan?" my wife offered kindly. On the buffet, alongside one wall, sputtered a black table fan, letting out a barely discernable breeze as it spun in one direction, then, after hiccupping a little stop-and-start-again gasp, turned back the other way.

"Oh, thank goodness you noticed that," Lottie said, her voice going up a few levels in alarm. "Clem, turn that fan off, will you? That chilled air is no good for the baby!"

Clem sprang toward the offending fan and switched it off.

Once Clem took his seat again, Lottie said, "Now, let's all take our places and say Grace."

*　　*　　*

"Enough, enough!" I protested.

There is no polite way to refuse food in a Polish household, and while there are impolite ways, they are no more effective.

I looked down on my plate, where thick, glistening kielbasa sausages nestled on top of the boiled potatoes that were smothering the stuffed cabbage. Bending over my shoulder from behind was Lottie, ladling another trio of kraut-and-mushroom pierogies onto my plate.

"You should feed this boy more at home," she said to my wife. "Then he wouldn't be so bashful when he goes out."

"Aunt Lottie, why don't you sit down and eat something yourself?" my wife asked our hostess.

"Oh, don't you worry about me—I want to make sure there's enough food for everyone else first. Oh, that reminds me—I almost forgot!"

She hurried into the kitchen, and I could hear the refrigerator door open. Was she actually going to bring out something that had been kept cool?

"I almost forgot the salad," she said, as she brought out a platter with a jiggling sculpture of yellow and green. "Have some Jell-O® salad: It's nice and light," she said, carving into the ring-shaped mold with a serving spoon. "It's lemon and lime Jell-O with green cabbage and carrots and sour cream. It will clean your palate before more pork roast."

The heat and the heavy food and the warm cream soda and the dinnertime conversation were making me feel queasy. Clem had been reminiscing about the old days, when he and Lottie lived on the farm and made what he said was the best headcheese in all of South Bend, thanks to the tasty pigs they raised. "You use everything but the oink," he joked. They talked about their award-winning garden, a project that won the top prize from the Ladies Auxiliary of Saint Stanislaus parish. Their hydrangea bushes were taller and wider than any hydrangeas had a right to be, Clem added, and were covered each summer with an embarrassing richness of blooms.

"What's the secret?" I asked.

"The kitchen scraps," Clem said. "Plants like to eat good, too, you know. They get the potato peels and the cabbage ends and the coffee grounds. We don't waste anything. Are you going to clean your plate?" he asked me, pointing to the chunks of fat I had cut away from the beef roast and the pork roast and the veal roast. "If not, we'll put that in the slop pot. We don't raise pigs any more, but old Mr. Krakowski still has his farm just outside of town. His porkers love our leftovers."

Much as I feared the bathroom encounter, there was no more putting it off. Two hours in the car with lots of iced tea along the way, the warm soda on top of it and a few glasses of lukewarm water to wash down the taste of that soda had completely filled up my bladder. I excused myself and took the three steps to the bathroom. I put my hand on the door and tentatively pushed it open a few feet.

I walked in and closed the door behind me, then crossed over to the door that led to the kitchen and closed that also. I took a deep breath and surveyed the room. It was big and damp and gloomy. Next to the bathtub, a glass block window high up above a white cabinet with chipping enamel let in a feeble stream of light.

I warily turned my glance toward the toilet. It looked normal enough. I glanced at the wall. No sign saying "Just in case." I looked beside the toilet and saw a thick yellow plastic wastebasket. Leaning inside was the just-in-case stick. I approached it warily, like a character in an old silent movie, moving my feet slowly and deliberately, as if sneaking up on it. I leaned over to examine it. The stick was a foot-long wooden ruler. Printed in the middle of the inch markings it read, "Golonka's Sausage Shoppe and Hair Salon."

Yuck. Just what I did not want to see, an advertisement for what sounded like a butcher shop that doubled as a beauty parlor.

I had to go. I put the pink padded foam toilet seat up—while listening to the dinner table conversation outside the door. Lottie was saying, "I always keep a few extra cans of evaporated milk in my pantry because you never know when you might have a cooking emergency."

I did not want everyone to hear my big rush of fluids, so I put the seat back down and took my place on it, which I knew would make less noise. As I emptied my bladder, I began to realize how childish and even mean-spirited I was being. Here I was, judging these people for not updating their bathroom or their way of living when in fact I was the one who was out of touch with life's natural processes. After all, what's the big deal? Everyone has the same bodily functions, right?

I got up from the toilet and turned on the faucet marked "cold." Warm water rushed out. As I washed my hands, I looked at myself in the mirror and was surprised how bloated and blotchy my face looked.

The relief I finally felt in my bladder had freed up my mind to concentrate on the fact that I had just spent the last hour in a 110-degree house stuffing myself with fat and grease from various meat products, along with cabbage-laced Jell-O, while being regaled with pig-slaughtering stories. I had to burp. Or something.

I needed to get out of this house. I jerked open the door to the kitchen and saw Diane coming in with some dirty dishes from the dining room.

"Are you okay?" she asked, which seemed odd, since she looked like she was about to birth a baby any second.

"Yeah," I said, "I just need to take a few deep breaths. Guess I ate too much."

Think of something else, I told myself. I saw a large earthenware jug on the counter. It had a mottled earthy golden color with a little floral design.

"That's nice," I said. "What is it—a pickle jar?"

I walked over and started to pick up the lid.

"Jeez, Jim, I wouldn't do that if I were you," Diane said.

Too late. I was staring into a bubbling cauldron of kitchen waste. As I realized I couldn't identify what kind of chunks were bobbing on the surface, I began to gag. It was the slop pot.

"Oh, God, Jim, I told you not to look," Diane said. "Go outside. Get some air!"

She yanked open the back door. I ran to the hydrangeas, where I bent over and did what nature compelled me to do.

A few minutes later, I felt much better. It helped that it was so much cooler outside; the big wall thermometer on the shed read only 99 degrees.

I took a few deep breaths and walked up the wooden porch steps and back into the kitchen.

"Are you okay?" Diane asked, clearly concerned.

"Yeah," I said. "Just embarrassed." I was happy she was alone in the kitchen. "I hope Lottie and Clem won't be upset if they find out what I did in their hydrangeas."

"Where do you think this is going?" Diane asked, pointing to the slop pot, which was now filled to the top. "If anything, you just saved them another trip."

Just then, Lottie leaned her head into the kitchen.

"We left your plate on the table, Jim," she said. "I've got two more nice big pieces of kielbasa with your name on them!"

Morning Rituals

by Barbara Moriarty

The idea that a family of eight could share the same bath seems crazy to me now, but in 1967 it was, well, normal. There was no sunken tub or Boston ferns, no surround sound stereo or rainfall showerhead—just a single white sink, a toilet or commode as Aunt Karen called it, and a glorious tub. All this tucked into a 4' by 7' space that Dad and a fireman friend had tiled in speckled white and blue ceramic. A wallpaper of forget-me-not flowers spilled across the upper walls. White, as I later learned, makes everything appear larger than it really is, or is that childhood? No matter, somehow that bathroom still looms large in my memory.

We had rules: if you showered, which was discouraged in order to maintain the clean look of the hand-tiled ceramic, you had to use a squeegee on the walls when done. Kids were not allowed to swing from the towel bars, a lesson I learned one day after crashing into the sink as the towel bar gave way, leaving me with an apple-sized bruise on my knee. No more gymnastics in the house I promised. Put the dirty towels in the hamper. Last but not least: be considerate of others and clean the tub. Dad always said he knew when it was my turn to clean because I'd leave a layer of cleanser clinging like beach sand to the porcelain tub bottom. To make bath time work, there had to be a system and a schedule, as well as a way around it if necessary.

At around 6:15 a.m. each day, Dad's alarm clock would go off and he'd sprint up the stairs, taking them two at a time to begin his morning ritual. First you'd hear the sink water running, followed by the "whoosh, whoosh" sound of his hands gathering water and rinsing his face of shaving cream, followed by alien snorts, gurgles and coughs, followed by a loud clink and the slurp of water draining then—nothing. The antique clock in the dining room gonged; it was 6:30.

Without a murmur, wearing her fuzzy slippers, Aunt Karen shuffled out of our room. She traded places with Dad and started her shower. It ran hard for about seven minutes, which felt like an hour when you were 10 and trying not to worry about the math homework that you didn't quite finish the night before. Again, things got quiet. I'd relax and start to doze off again only to be awakened by the pssst, pssst—shots of hairspray that would envelope the bedroom and bring me out of my dreams. Then, in full makeup and hair that wouldn't move in a windstorm, Karen went to start a bath for my brothers.

"Mike, time to get up for school," Aunt Karen whispered

as she shook my brother's shoulder.

"In a minute... All right, all right I'm going. Why doesn't he go first?" Mike said, jutting his chin toward our younger brother Bryan, asleep in the next bed.

"I took a bath last night," Bryan smiled to himself and then rolled over.

"Oh man!" Mike said, throwing off his covers.

Mike had a twice-weekly paper route and could be extra crabby the mornings he could sleep in a bit. He was nothing if not fast though, and would be in and out of the bathroom within ten minutes. Almost always, I merely pretended to be asleep while wondering if my little sister was still sleeping. Susan slept across the hall with our baby brother and I felt so envious that she got to keep the door closed.

Eyes still shut; I waited to hear the door slam open, which signaled my turn for ten minutes in the bathroom. The bang usually woke the baby, too, and then the wailing would start and Mom would run upstairs.

"Who's in that crib? Where's my baby?" she would coo.

Mike didn't bother to empty the tub, bubbles hiding any grime and I slipped in. Susan would trail behind me and stand on her tiptoes at the sink to reach her toothbrush. I'd watch her make faces like a fish, pursing her lips together, then opening to bare all her teeth in an exaggerated motion. There would be more toothpaste on the sink and her pajamas than anywhere else, and then the giggling would start.

"Susie!"

Mom would knock on the door. "What's going on in there, girls?"

"Naathingg," we'd sing out in unison, half holding our breath and exhaling in laughter only as we heard her footsteps fade down the hall.

Meanwhile, both brothers pulled out their uniform blue cotton shirts and navy ties from the closet. Just knowing our mother was two feet behind them made them move faster. The sound of their feet rumbling down the staircase let me know bath time was over.

"Stop hitting me," Bryan said.

"Did not," Mike answered.

"Did too, loser."

In an hour and some change, two adults were ready for work and four of five kids were at the breakfast table clamoring over cereal boxes. I'm not sure when my mother got a chance to shower. She seemed to perpetually be wearing a robe. The closest she ever came to a spa experience was when one of us ran our water too hot and turned the bathroom into a steam room.

If you think it was tough to choreograph bathroom time around the family—loo sharing reached new heights when we had visitors. One spring, Uncle Adolph and his wife Judy drove from Pennsylvania to Chicago for their honeymoon. They slept on the pullout couch in the recreation room downstairs and sometime in the pale dawn, Judy took over our bath. One by one, we awoke to a closed bathroom door. We didn't hear a peep. The band of light at the bottom of the doorway was our only clue that the room was inhabited.

Our mother warned us not to knock or bother her in any way. So we waited while hopping about as we held our bladders in.

I remember staring at her beehive hairstyle the night before at dinner and wondering out loud how she got all that hair piled up with tendrils framing the sides of her face.

"You have to rat it and spray it," Aunt Karen answered, running her hand over her teased blonde updo.

Judy's false eyelashes, shadowed eyelids and peach lipstick were amazing to me because my mother never wore any makeup. Such beauty took time to achieve—lots of time—in our one and only bathroom.

We ate cereal, watched cartoons and even made our beds. Still the door remained shut. Just when we were ready to bust, Judy emerged. She'd been in there 45 minutes. Now, she had her train case in hand as she floated past the entire family, like a runway model for JC Penney. Uncle Adolph stood there in his lumberjack shirt, hands shoved deep into the back pockets of his jeans, giving her an adoring gaze. He spun around and followed his bride back to the honeymoon suite in the rec room.

It might seem as though our entire our family life revolved around getting in and out of the bathroom in record setting time each day. The tension eased during the summer months and on weekends when swimming lessons at the YMCA and summer camp gave us options. The force of air from those wall mounted hair dryers could dry and straighten hair in no time flat. Our teen years, however, called for more creative thinking. My brother Bryan and I always seemed to need the bathroom at the same time. Once, I started the warm water running and he decided I'd drawn a bath for him.

"Hey," I yelled pounding on the door as he soaped up inside.

"Sorry," he answered in a nasal tone, "It's the team's picture night, you know—before the dance. Are you going?"

"Arrggh... That's why I was running a bath."

Not to be outfoxed again, I took to adding a capful of Avon's Skin So Soft® bath oil into the tub. That alone didn't stop Bryan from stealing my next bath, but taunts and whistles from his football buddies about his heavenly scent and glistening skin solved my problem for good.

Eventually, we got some relief when Aunt Karen married and moved out, followed by Dad putting a summer shower in the basement. With four teens taking two showers a day it was the only practical thing to do, and as the gaps in our school and social schedules grew wider negotiating bathroom time was a skill we refined to an art.

We passed in and out of that room wearing all the costumes of young adulthood for proms, graduations and weddings. The downside of my experiences made me slightly neurotic about bathrooms without locks. It took years for me to get over the feeling that someone could unexpectedly burst into the bathroom at any moment— even after I had moved out.

Today, my bath is my sanctuary, complete with a deep tub, candles and yes, a rainfall showerhead. It's peaceful, no one bothers me and I wouldn't trade it for anything. Or so I thought until recently.

Last month, I visited my younger brother who has three kids: ages two, four and six. All three were telling me about their lives: Bodies and sentences overlapped like a modern dance troupe for tots as we made our way into the house. While using their powder room, my older niece slipped her school picture through the crack in the door, continuing her story of what she wore that day. Without warning, her younger sister and brother started opening the door and I had to jerk the handle back to keep the crowd at bay. We went tug of war with the door for another minute until it closed with a thud.

"Guys, I'll be out in a minute," I pleaded. I could hear my brother calling their names from the kitchen and it brought me back to the crazy, chaotic fun of sharing a bath at a time of my life that's irreplaceable.

Towel bar gym, anyone?

Hot Water

by Barbara Moriarty

It was October. The Great Smoky Mountains National Park was a golden paradise of autumn colors at every turn. I sighed, relieved to be 700 miles away from the corporate buyout that had cost me my job and also the late night calls from my sister who was in the midst of her divorce. A change of scenery was what I needed: a cabin in the woods, dinner in a rustic dining room next to a roaring fireplace and a steeping hot shower after a long day's hike. You know, the kind that fogs the mirror and turns the edges of your ears pink. To me, nothing could be more soothing or invigorating than a shower. And, if I had to do a little hiking to get there, well, I'd deal with it.

Jeff, a new friend, parked our van at a lookout point and the five of us spilled out of its doors, limp from sitting in the same paralyzing position for over six hours.

"Whew," I said, thrilled to stand up straight after driving all day from Kentucky to Tennessee.

"Made it," said Linda, a friend since high school, while stretching her hands to her toes, her blond ponytail flipping over and bouncing against her knees. We looked straight out at the mountains where giant green patches of pine trees covered their peaks and rested against a backdrop of blue sky. The valley below resembled an Impressionist painting awash in a sea of yellow, orange and red brushstrokes.

"Hey, let's get a picture," Jerry said, removing his army sweatshirt to reveal broad shoulders and a trim waist.

"I'll take it, you get in the picture," I ordered, grabbing the camera. They all jockeyed around for a minute, and finally fell into a boy-girl pattern. Jerry scooted in next to Bonnie, an accountant, and stretched his arm across her back hooking her tiny waist. Bonnie had mentioned she liked to run in the mornings before work and the fitness team logo on her tee shirt confirmed it.

With the exception of Linda, who had invited me, I didn't know anyone in this group. But I'll tell you this—they were in shape—not a ripple or ounce of fat on any one of them. As I squinted through the camera lens and they smiled back, I knew I was out of my league. My hobbies were eating out and shopping. Instinctively, I knew that this was not their first hiking trip, but it was mine. There was no turning back as home was a 15-hour drive back to Chicago.

"Cheese," I yelled.

Jeff wanted to go on a practice hike to a spot called Chimleys and see the sunset before heading to his mother's house in Tyron, North Carolina. The leaves crunched beneath my feet and I was retelling the story of my layoff to Jerry when we happened on to a sign that read, "No hikers beyond this point." To the left was a slat ladder built into the flat side of a hill—straight up. Jeff pulled work gloves out of his jacket pockets and began handing them out. I stared at him in disbelief. "Are you really going up there?" I asked, heart pounding.

"You'll see. It's really pretty and the best part of the trip," he said, thrusting the canvas gloves toward me. I folded my arms across my chest and shook my head. My eyes grew narrow as his opened wider, neither one of us willing to budge.

"Take these," he added, the corners of his mouth turned up slightly, "in case you change your mind." My desire to see the sunset from a mountain disappeared, as I was sure I didn't want to go home in a body cast.

"See you guys later," I said and turned around to walk back to the parking lot. I couldn't wait to have a cigarette. No one on this trip knew I smoked, really I intended to quit—after I found a new job, of course. As I leaned against the strong back of an oak tree and puffed, I couldn't help but notice a long black hump on a tree a few hundred feet ahead of me. It was a bear sleeping peacefully on a long branch.

In that instant, I didn't know if I should be scared, so for moment, I just stood there in awe gaping at Mr. Grizzly. I contemplated moving in closer to get a better look; maybe just to be sure it was really a bear. But what could I offer him if he awoke and was hungry—a little tobacco maybe? Surely this sighting could top anything my hiker friends were seeing on top of the mountain. Playing it safe, I stubbed my cigarette out, ran back to the van and pushed the lock buttons on the inside doors. Sinking down low in the bench seat I reviewed the day: "Damn hiking trip, why didn't I go to a spa instead?"

The shower at Jeff's mom's place that night was amazing. I stayed in the bathroom a long time letting the hot water soothe my back muscles. Afterward, the thick terry towels made me feel like a small child all wrapped up in warmth. These hot showers were saving my life. I had worked for the same company for 11 years and loved it, but now that was gone. My freelance writing assignments were more fascinating than lucrative and I was broke with no good prospects in site. I was literally a month away from moving back home with my parents, a grim prospect after being on my own for so many years. Turning in early seemed like the best decision in anticipation of our hiking day, and so I said goodnight to my friends.

Despite a couple of regrets from the previous day, I awoke refreshed and ready to start hiking early the next day. We hadn't been hiking long before my face had turned beet red as I made the climb on the Alum Cave Trail, which was six miles upward ending at an altitude of 6,593 feet. Although I didn't know it at the time, this was the steepest of the five trails offered by the National Park. Still looking like a ripe tomato, I tried to control my shallow breathing as we ascended.

Keep going, you can do it, my inner voice told me. My inexperience was evident by the full-size backpack I carried, which was twice as large as the other hikers and already raising havoc with my shoulders.

The extra room in my pack wasn't lost on Jeff who sheepishly asked me to carry a few of his toiletries, so he could fit another bottled water into his waist pack. I was wiping the perspiration from my forehead and losing complete confidence in my abilities when after the first mile and a half, the trail leveled out.

We sat down and unwrapped the ham and cheese sandwiches we'd made that morning and I started telling Jeff the story of my layoff, hoping to get a different perspective or at least some empathy as I caught my breath.

"I think you're really going to like LeConte Lodge," he said, not knowing how to respond to my joblessness, and too polite to tell me he already heard the story in the van. "They do a really nice job with dinner: pot roast and potatoes with gravy and peach cobbler for dessert. Everything gets carried up there by llamas a couple times a week. There's a lounge where you can read or another hike we can go on to see the moon rise not far from the lodge," he added. He was killing me with these excursions. All I wanted was that shower he promised me on the driveway back in Chicago.

"Oh, I can't wait," I said, standing up to take in the sight of birds flying in formation over a band of red spruce trees.

Jeff was right, the view was awesome, and the only sound I heard was of birds singing and the wind. My legs and back muscles were aching; nothing a hot shower and a good night's sleep wouldn't cure, however.

As we returned to the trail, I developed a quicker pace. I even smiled, then grimaced while holding onto the cable wires strung between the rocks on a narrow cleft, insurance to keep hikers from falling off the open slope. We got closer to the lodge at Cliff Tops as the sun was setting and walked past a six-foot-high link fence. "What's that?" I asked, despite the obvious.

"Oh, that fence. It keeps the campers safe from the bears at night," Jeff said.

"Thank God we've got our rooms," I answered, visualizing a separate cozy bathroom cabin complete with showers and maybe a warm wood sauna. I still wanted to smoke, but didn't dare, now that I felt like I was starting to earn my group's respect as a hiker.

The shingled rooftops of the cabins and the lodge came into view and I snapped a shot of my group heading in toward civilization. Our timing was perfect; I wanted to get washed up before dinner. "Jeff, which way to the showers?" I asked.

"Right there," he pointed to a small shed that looked like, you guessed it, an outhouse.

" Oh, c'mon! Where's the hot shower you promised me," I pleaded unable to accept my fate.

"Unless you want me to pour a bucket of water over your head, that's it, Babe."

I felt the blood rush to my face making it hot and suddenly I was filled with the desire to throw something at Jeff and knock that baseball cap off his head. He stood there grinning from ear to ear holding his arm crooked over his face—a wise move since he was about to be hit with one of his own toiletries that I'd so graciously carted up the mountainside for him.

" Sorry," Jeff said sheepishly as he started race walking toward our cabin.

I dropped my pack onto the ground and started to laugh. The pressure I'd been feeling started to melt and I laughed harder letting my knees give way and tumbled down to the ground. It really was crazy to think there'd be a hot steamy shower and sauna at a place where llamas trek and bears hibernate, that along with the idea that Jeff might now be afraid of me made me howl. Dinner was going to be interesting.

Where I Sit

by William D. Hicks

This where we sit
Me, myself, I
Pondering life
On throne
Do this right?
Do that wrong?
Who be?
Who want be?
Why that person famous?
Why not we?
Be there God?
Life full of crap?
So full, we smell it...
But wait...
We in bathroom...
We be smelling we?
Life that stinky?
Maybe.

Section Six: When Love Leads to Hot Water

From the Desk of Mr. Man-ners

Dear Mr. Man-ners:

At a recent White House dinner with the Bushes, I found myself powdering my nose while waiting to use one of the 35 bathrooms in that magnificent mansion. As I reflected on my good fortune to be in such wonderful company, I overheard two women discussing their favorite Democratic choices (you heard me right) for our next president. I was aghast. Tell me, is it in poor taste to mention the opposite political party while dining with members of the current party? Honestly, what if Laura or, worse, Barbara Bush had been in the room?

Dumbfounded by Dems

Dear Dumbfounded by Dems:

First off, these women weren't dining; they were at the other end, so to speak, of the process. Now, for the question at hand. I'm aghast! There are 35 restrooms in the White House and you still had to wait in line? Were the others all occupied—or did you have to use that special one with a life-size portrait of Ronald Reagan? Or perhaps the reason they were all full is because most politicians are full of it (you know what I mean). You're asking all the wrong questions here. Who cares if people were speaking about voting for the opposite political party? Who cares about how Laura or Barbara would feel if they heard such talk? Do you think they're stupid? It's not like either of their husbands can get re-elected to the office. The real question is; how can the White House host a fancy soiree when we're in the middle of a recession and gas prices are over $4 per gallon and millions of people are out of work? Oh yeah, that's right, the Bushes own oil.

Mr. Man-ners

Tête-à-Tête
by Barbara Yohnka

She checked her watch, noting it was already 8:15 p.m. She wondered why he could never show up on time. She glanced at the menu. The prime rib looked good. She checked her watch again. Why did she put up with his continual tardiness? It was a control issue, she thought.

The waiter came by and asked if she wanted a drink.

"Jack Daniels® on the rocks," she said, placing the menu face down on the table.

"Did you want to order for your party, too?" he asked.

"No, he can order his own damn drink." The waiter raised his eyebrows.

She sat back in the cushioned booth. She loved this restaurant; it was classy and cool and had the best steaks. And their chocolate mousse was to die for. This place was one of their favorite rendezvous.

She glanced around at the other people seated near her. Most of them were couples, but there were a few women, obviously on the prowl, sipping their drinks provocatively, slipping their pink tongues out to capture the straw that supplied the nectar that fed their confidence. She was just like them before she met him—available, searching, eager to please.

However, from the moment they got together, her prowling stopped and the only one she looked for was he: At her door. At her table. In her bed. She had been eager and delighted to see him. Yet, when he became complacent, started taking her time for granted, and stopped calling when he said he would, it was her style to become less available.

It was hard work being "unavailable," but it was a relief to not be at his beck and call. Once he realized that she could be as cavalier as he was, their roles reversed. He became the eager one, and she was the one he wanted to please.

"Here's your drink, Miss," the waiter said, placing a napkin and the drink on the table. She stirred the amber liquid, hearing the ice crack as the whiskey mingled with it.

That's what I should be doing, she thought, mingling. She looked at her watch—8:30. That's it. I'm done waiting for him. I'll order something to go, finish my drink at the bar and go home.

Having made up her mind, she garnered the waiter's attention, placed her order for prime rib, baked potato with the works, and a salad with their house honey lemon dressing. No reason she couldn't still enjoy a good meal.

Tucking her blonde hair behind her left ear, she

clutched her purse, smoothed her skirt, picked up her drink and the napkin, and sidled out of the booth. She was glad she'd worn the wedges; not only were they comfortable but they made her legs look good. Then she walked to the bar, found a stool and perched on the seat, trying to delicately balance herself, the drink and her purse. Before she could steady herself, her purse took a nosedive off the bar and she reactively tried to grab it in mid fall, almost tumbling off the stool.

"I'll get that!" a voice said, grabbing the purse and righting her tipping chair.

"Thanks! I needed another hand," she said, glancing up at the man. Her face flushed as she surveyed his, noting the dimples in his left cheek, the stubble of beard on his chin, the salt and pepper curls that framed his ear, and the hair that peeked near the top of his light blue polo shirt. She exhaled, realizing she'd been holding her breath.

"Thanks again," she said, quickly sipping her drink, her mouth suddenly desert dry. He smiled. "Perhaps I can buy you a drink," she said, "I'm waiting for my order."

"That'd be nice," he replied, sitting beside her. He took a napkin from the spiraled stack on the bar, and raised his hand for the bartender who took his order—Jack Daniels® on the rocks—while she checked out the rest of the package. He was muscular, but not ostentatious, and his blue shirt was tucked neatly into a pair of flat front dark brown khakis. He was probably a golfer; she saw the telltale tan lines on his arms. His hands were long and lean, a sign of...

"Do you come here often?" he asked. "That sounded like your typical come-on, didn't it?" He laughed. Those damn dimples.

She giggled. "I suppose, and yes, I do. This is one of my favorite restaurants."

"You're not waiting for someone?" he asked.

"I was, but I'm not anymore. Lots of couples here."

"I wonder how they stay together," he said, curiously.

"I think you have to work on it; bring some spice into the relationship. After a while I'd think it would get stale. Same man. Or woman. Every night. Every day. Perhaps..."

"Perhaps you have to do the unexpected," he said, sidling closer to her. "Now this is where you say..."

"This is where I say, follow me." She downed her drink, grabbed her purse, took his hand, and led him across the dining area, past the billiard room, and down a long hall. When she came to the sign that read "Ladies," she tried the door, found it unlocked, and pulled him inside.

Bolting the door on the inside, she put her arms around his neck and planted a kiss on his smiling lips.

"So this is what a women's restroom looks like," he said, glancing around the room. His eyes settled on the expansive counter that held a number of toiletries. He pushed the items away, picked her up and placed her on the counter. Then he pulled up her blouse, dropped the cups of her bra and massaged her breasts.

"I like it. They should do this for men," he said, nibbling her neck.

"Did you notice the couch?"

"That's convenient." He sucked one breast into his mouth.

She unbuckled his belt, pulled up his shirt, and then ran her fingers through the hair that shaded his chest. His nipples puckered.

She tightened her embrace, twirled her tongue through his ear, and whispered, "Let's move to the couch."

He lifted her up (she always wanted a man who could do that!), reached under her skirt, and pulled her towards him.

"You're ready," she said, grinding her hips against his.

"You too. Come here."

He sat on the sofa, unzipped his pants, drew aside her panties, and placed her on his lap like she was a candle on a cake. They were so totally immersed in tasting and touching one another that they didn't hear the door handle jiggle, nor the staccato of knocks that followed. Someone banged loudly on the door a second time and she called out, "I've got an emergency here! Try the men's room," she said, and stuffed a breast in his mouth to keep him from laughing.

"Quick thinking."

"I've used that line before," she replied, bouncing on his lap.

"We're almost there," he said, "just wait for it," sucking

her lower lip into his mouth. A few minutes later, after several satisfying sighs, she tucked in her breasts and straightened her skirt while he zipped himself and his shirt into his pants.

"Hope our food's ready," she said, fixing his collar. "I'm unexpectedly starved for meat."

"And speaking of unexpected," he chuckled, "how cool of you to think of ordering dinner too. Let's go home, honey," he said, kissing her cheek, "and finish what we started."

Room for Doubt

by Barbara Moriarty

Mary Helen was locked in the master bathroom. It was her wedding day, a perfect day in June, and one that she thought she'd never experience again. Still in her robe, but already made-up and hair styled, she knew she had only to step into that wedding dress to change her life. Her sister Maureen was pounding on the door and her cell phone was vibrating its way across the cherry wood surface of the dressing table. Mary Helen's fears about marriage paralyzed her as she sat on a velvet-tufted cushion adjacent to the table with a washcloth draped across her forehead, waiting for something to change—a sign from God or even her late mother—anything that might pull her up and out of here.

She was 74 years old, for Pete's sake.

Just an hour earlier Mary Helen had stood in front of her antique brass bed admiring the ivory brocade suit spread across the quilted comforter. She lifted its hem and rubbed her thumb across the fabric. The peplum jacket was soft to the touch as was the matching slim skirt. She loved the way the gold threads ran through the floral design and how the skirt hit her leg mid-knee. Hal, her betrothed, always said she had great legs and the thought made her smile as she envisioned herself walking down the church aisle escorted by her eldest son, David, a Chicago attorney.

Hal, the new love of her life, was four years older, just enough to make her feel like the younger half of his other half, as corny as that sounded. He had surprised her with a ring tied to a soupspoon at Cesario's Italian Restaurant last spring. Hell, he'd even gone down on one knee (granted the waiters had to help him back up) before popping the question. Cesario's was their favorite neighborhood place and they'd gone there for dinner every other Saturday since they started dating nine months earlier. After she said yes, tears and mascara streaming down her cheeks, everyone in the place cheered.

At the insistence of Hal's daughter Jennifer, from his second marriage, their engagement picture appeared on the social page of the Janesville Reporter alongside pictures of couples half their age or those with decades-long anniversaries.

Mary Helen had been divorced for 23 years and although things were tough when the children were in school, she never regretted her decision— if you could call it that. Her first husband, Dale, had run off to Vegas with her best friend, Doris, and that pretty much decided the future of her marriage. There were no warning signs or perhaps she missed seeing them because she was too busy working part-time at the college library plus ironing Dale's seven cotton shirts each week (the ones that matched his suits), not to mention vacuuming and serving up meals gleaned from Fannie Farmer's cookbook recipes. It was years before she could hear anyone mention Las Vegas or the name Doris Delfry without her stomach turning.

Make no mistake; Mary Helen was pleased with her life. She had her children—three boys, and her books—a whole library of them where she escaped nightly. But life had caught her off guard when she and Hal starting meeting for decaf coffee after their Yoga for Seniors class at the community center. Although they each took up yoga for very different reasons it was the first common thread between them. At the advice of her counselor, Mary Helen began twisting her body into a pretzel to help manage her anxiety after she'd heard about Dale's heart attack and subsequent divorce from Doris. She was sure the hang-up calls she was getting in the middle of the night were from him and feared he might move back into town.

Hal, on the other hand, was simply following doctor's orders to use yoga as part of his physical therapy after knee replacement surgery. Thank the Lord.

Twenty-three years was a long time to be alone and this empty nester found she still had had a lot of love to give. Hal, a retired carpenter with a penchant for making planters out of discarded toilet bowls, made her heart skip a beat (although she thought it was her micro valve prolapse) when he first locked eyes with her from his yoga mat three rows over. The planters he made were beautiful, she thought. Hal gifted her with one painted with a copper finish and filled with pansies. It looked like it always belonged in the spot next to the oak tree in her garden.

Was she actually getting married again today or was it a dream? None of it seemed real until now. Mary Helen pulled her to-do list from her robe's pocket. The family was to be at her house at 1:30 p.m. Working backwards meant she only had half an hour left to put on her face and get dressed before the photographer arrived.

The grandfather clock downstairs began to chime just as her phone rang again. It was her neighbor asking about the house key. "Yes, Alice, I'll leave the key in the planter. Yes, the toilet shaped one. Okay, bye, bye." No sooner had she replaced the receiver on the nightstand phone than her cell phone, still in her purse in the bathroom, started chirping. Then, the doorbell rang. Stay calm, she thought. It's just Alice's daughter coming to fill the punch bowl and set out hors d'oeuvres for after the ceremony.

"C'mon in, Sweetie," Mary Helen yelled down the stairs pulling the terry fabric tight against her chest. Her cell phone had stopped, then started again. The bride was getting rattled. She wasn't used to the phones going crazy or all the commotion. Since the boys moved out she had grown accustomed to her quiet place and had not missed picking up dirty socks or asking anyone to turn the music down. She hoped Hal picked up his clothes at home. He had a cleaning woman so it was hard to know his habits.

The wedding was at 3 p.m. at the Village Presbyterian Church a few miles away. She and Hal had decided to keep the ceremony small, intimate really, with just their very best friends and immediate family. Their yoga instructor would be there, of course, because she "shared their joy." Mary Helen walked to the bathroom and flipped her phone open. "Hello?"

"Mary Helen, I'm here!" screeched her younger sister Maureen.

Mary Helen held the phone a foot from her ear before responding sweetly, "Maureen, it's wonderful to hear your voice. How was your flight?"

"Well, we were delayed for over an hour, but we flew first class on our frequent flyer miles. Jealous?"

"Maureen, you like Hal, don't you?" she asked, hoping for absolute reassurance.

"I guess so. No, I do. Why would you even think...Oh, here's Ed now with the Lincoln Towncar—another upgrade. See 'ya in 20, Doll."

She heard the kissing sound that was always Maureen's signoff.

"I love you too," she answered, more to herself, as she clasped the phone shut.

Now, looking at her reflection in the mirror, Mary Helen thought, Not bad, for an old lady. Her pale blonde hair was pulled up into a French twist, and a long bang fell across her forehead hiding a furrowed brow. Despite the wrinkles, her skin was flawless. Years of wearing sunhats while gardening had paid off. Mary Helen's hand began to tremble as she attempted to blot her lips with a tissue. Tears welled in her blue eyes and she ended up using the tissue to dab at them. "I can't marry him," she said out loud. "I have too much to lose."

Mary Helen walked over to the vanity and sank into the velvet cushion. Her skin was paler than usual and she couldn't understand the wave of nausea that suddenly overtook her. "Dear God, I'm getting the flu. I have to call Hal to tell him."

She called his cell phone and let it ring seven times. Thank goodness her grandson had programmed her address book so she could just press a button. No answer. "The caller you are trying to reach has not set up voicemail service," the recording said.

"Oh, Hal, where are you?" Mary Helen muttered. Well, there was nothing to do other than call her sister whom, while never good in a crisis, was certain to get the word out to the relatives. She pressed the phone's keys with shaking hands.

"Maureen, it's me. Listen, I'm sick," she whispered. "I can't get married today."

"Did you take your pills? You know how you get when you haven't eaten. And, why are you whispering for God's sake? Mary Helen, we're here for you, me and Eddy all the way from Scottsdale," Maureen protested.

"Can you go to Hal's and tell him? He's not answering the phone—please."

"Sis, what's wrong? It's been a long time since Dale left you. I promise it won't happen like that again. When I think of what that man did to you..." Maureen began to cry.

Mary Helen heard the tires screech followed by the sound of muffled voices. Her stomach did a flip-flop. She could hear her brother-in-law calling her name just as her body went limp and she crumpled onto the cool tile of the bathroom floor, phone still in hand.

"Listen Mary Helen, this is Ed, I'm parking the car and we'll discuss this. Don't you worry 'bout anything. There's nothing family can't help solve."

While she could admit that he might have a point, the dubious bride was now on her knees with her head tipped over the toilet bowl.

*   *   *

Outside the house, Maureen and Ed rushed up the sidewalk to the front door of two-story brick Colonial and rang the bell repeatedly.

"Do you think she has any of that whiskey left from Christmas?" Ed asked.

"Jesus, Mary and Joseph! My sister is on the brink of ruining her life and all you've got on your mind is whiskey?" Maureen said, waving and smiling at the teenage girl who approached the door carrying a punch bowl and wearing jeans tight enough to cut off the circulation in most people. "Hello, dear, you must be Alice's daughter, but I've misplaced your name," Maureen said.

"I'm Amy," she answered snapping her gum. "Is Mrs. O'Halleran home? I'm supposed to make the punch."

"And I'm here to help," Ed winked. His wife gave him a shove. Ed still liked to tango with the ladies, even though he was pushing 70 and looked every bit of it, suit or no suit.

"Have you got a key, dear? I'm afraid my sister isn't answering, pre-wedding jitters and all," Maureen said, banging the brass knocker.

"I know she keeps one in the planter out back," Amy said setting the bowl down. She spun on her heel to lead them toward the backdoor. "Follow me. I'll get you in."

Meanwhile, upstairs, Mary Helen had managed to crawl over to the dressing table and was ringing Hal at home. No answer. She recalled that he had a haircut and shave appointment at Sammy's Barber Shop and called directory assistance for the number. It would be rude not to tell him that she decided to call things off.

"Sammy's," said the throaty male voice on the other end.

"Is Hal Donatucci there?" Mary Helen managed to squeak out.

"He is, but I've got him under the knife, Dumdum ta dum," the barber sang to the tune of, "Here Comes the Bride." She could hear Hal letting loose with laughter in the background and she hung up. She could just imagine her man sitting in the swivel chair, a white apron draped across his chest, telling Sammy about the wedding while the barber clipped away at Hal's silver waves—the feature that first attracted her to him. Oh, she couldn't ruin it for him. Now what?

The footsteps on the stairs startled Mary Helen and she pulled herself up. A quick glance in the vanity mirror revealed her time at the salon earlier that day had been wasted. Her hair was falling out of her updo and her face was a mess. "Good Lord, who's there?" she asked in response to the knock on the door. Her phone began vibrating across the vanity, but not before she saw the name Dale O'Halleran on her caller ID. Damn, that man was a nuisance, she thought. What the hell did he want? This was her wedding day—something else he planned to ruin? She let it ring without answering.

Outside the door, a very familiar voice called out, "Doll, it's me, your baby sister. Let me in so we can talk. Ed and the neighbor girl are downstairs and David's on the way. We passed him on the highway."

"Go away, Maureen. I'm not feeling well. You have no idea what I'm facing right now."

Maureen began pounding on the bathroom door with an open hand and Mary Helen turned on the water in response. The sisters had always competed with each other. Mary Helen had been the pretty blonde one, a majorette at Whitmore High. It was her picture that sat above the words "most popular" in the faded yearbook. And so it was quite a disappointment to have married badly and not fully recovered to this day.

Maureen, on the other hand, slightly overweight and having inherited their Uncle Connor's Scottish nose, never cared much about her appearance or her grades when they were young. Yet it was she who ended up with the loyal husband, (even if he did drink a bit) and a good job as an administrative assistant for the president of Yonkers Department store. Maureen and Ed lived quite comfortably in their Arizona ranch house, and although seemingly well meaning, never let her forget it.

While Mary Helen pondered her sister's good fortune in husbands, Maureen was drawn to the pink and green plaid satin slipper chair beside the bed. A soft breeze blowing through the window billowed the white chiffon curtains. "My dogs are barking," she said limping over to the chair, needing no further invitation to sit down. She had only just wrestled her swollen feet out of her patent pumps when David burst into the room.

"Mom! Mom, you're going to be late for your own wedding. Why aren't you ready yet? The photographer's going to be here any minute," he said, surveying the room and noticing his mother's dress on the bed.

"Hi David," Maureen said, waving her nephew toward the bathroom with one hand while continuing to rub her foot with the other.

David jiggled the glass doorknob. "Ma, it's two o'clock."

"Honey, I don't know," the now-wilted bride sighed loudly from behind the door. "I think I'm just too old to go through this marriage business again."

"Mom, what happened with Dad was years ago. Hal's great; he loves you," David said gingerly, raising his arms to his forehead and leaning his six-foot frame against the door.

Mary Helen started to cry. She knew it was true. "I let you down back then."

"No, Mom, you didn't," David said. "Scott and Brian don't feel that way either. If you tell me you're not happy with Hal, I'll help you walk away now, but I think you're making a mistake if you let this guy go."

"Maybe," she answered. Mary Helen was so proud of her sons. Although David had his father's strong jaw line and other fine features, he wasn't brash like Dale had been. David treated women with respect. He and his brothers were the greatest gifts Mary Helen had gotten from that marriage. She smiled. If only her counselor could hear her say that she'd be $120 richer this week.

Mary Helen began thinking of alternatives: She and Hal could live together. They might skip the wedding and just take the honeymoon trip, or, they could just go back to the way things were before the engagement and keep separate homes. Maybe, after a while, they could get married, but on a Tuesday afternoon, without all the fuss. She realized there were options. And, Hal, her best friend, her intended, was the only one who could make a plan with her.

Mary Helen unlocked the bathroom door and turned the handle. It was going to be all right. She had all the support she needed from her family, and besides that— she still wanted Hal in her life. She loved him.

David caught her in an embrace as she stepped out onto the soft carpet in the dressing room. He patted her on the back and loosened his hold on her. Mary Helen looked up at him and said, "You're a wonderful son."

By now Maureen was standing up holding her sister's wedding suit in her outstretched arms. "What do you think? Is there going to be a wedding after all?

"Well, I suppose it couldn't hurt to put on the dress. I paid enough for it," Mary Helen answered as she walked toward her sister.

Meanwhile, the doorbell had rung several times since David had come up. The sound of Ed's uproarious laughter and the clash of several voices carried upstairs. "I have to see what's going on down there," he announced.

As he bounced down the stairs, David could see the photographer setting up in the living room while his three-year old twin girls chased their cousin, Ren, who had just learned to walk, followed by Scamper, the Doberman Pincher belonging to Amy from next door. He began to clap his hands loudly to get everyone's attention, but the chaos continued into the kitchen. There at the table was red-faced Ed, who'd found the whiskey after all, recounting his days in the Navy to poor Amy, who was stirring an orange juice and ice cream concoction into her punch bowl. The look on her face strongly suggested she'd rather be elsewhere.

David's wife, Ann, was opening the back door off the kitchen for the groom, all suited and shaved, but who now looked somewhat anxious himself. He kissed Ann on the cheek. "Where's your mother?

"You know, Hal, it's bad luck to see the bride before the wedding."

"Funny thing happened, a friend of mine saw Dale at the barber shop this morning and I, uh well, has he been here?

"Who?"

"Dale, Mary Helen's ex."

Ann called over her shoulder to David. "Honey, I need you."

David and Hal shook hands, stepped forward to embrace, then, stepped back, finally ending in a half embrace with a lot of backslapping. "Hal, shouldn't you be at the church?"

"Your Dad's in town. Did you know?"

"I didn't. He's not invited to the wedding. I'm not sure he knows there is one."

"Well, I know your mother has been trying to reach me. So I thought I'd stop by. Oh, and I wanted to make sure you had the rings."

David patted the breast pocket of his suit. " Right here."

"Then, everything's fine," he went on, "Okay, tell Mary

Helen I'll see her at the church."

David let out a short laugh that sounded like a Canada goose snorting. His wife knew that laugh. It happened every time he was nervous or hiding something and she met his eyes with a steely gaze.

Ann turned to her husband. "What's up?"

"Mom is having doubts, she locked herself in the bathroom, but she's getting dressed now. Should be okay from here."

Hal walked out the door and bumped right into Scott and Brian, David's younger brothers on the patio. They fell into their own male bonding ritual of half dance, half back slapping.

Seeing this, Ann grabbed her husband's elbow. "Oh my God David! Don't let Hal leave. They have to talk. Go get him. I'll see how your mom is doing." Ann grabbed her little one as he darted into the kitchen and wrestled him arms and legs flailing against her hip.

The photographer was snapping candid shots of the twins as Ann passed through the living room. The bows had fallen off their blonde heads and one had spilled something down the front of her dress. She didn't have to bother going upstairs to rescue her mother-in-law as Mary Helen was already on the last stair and looked radiant in her gold and ivory suit. Aunt Maureen was right behind her carrying her shoes. This was a good sign.

"Did I hear Hal?" Mary Helen asked.

"You did, and you must hear more," Ann said, jostling baby Ren while pointing to the back door with her one free hand. Mary Helen looked out the window and saw all the important men in her life were gathered on the patio. Hal sat on the stone bench in the center and seemed to be nodding his head to everything David was saying. Then he looked toward the house and spotted Mary Helen at the window. He stood up and waved.

She could no longer contain herself and hurried through the kitchen past Ed, who was dancing with Maureen, stepping over the Doberman and into the arms of the best man she had ever known. Her sons had vanished and at last it was just the two of them. "Let's get out of here," Hal said, pressing his lips against hers.

Mary Helen took his hand. "Where to?"

"I don't know. We'll see when we get there."

"But what about the wedding? Hal, I'm paying a photographer and my entire family..." she went on.

"Your entire family is crazy, including your ex, who may be on his way over, but fortunately for me they love you enough to let you go. The boys just gave me their blessing. Are you leaving with me or not?"

"Yes, I am Hal Donatucci."

Hal and Mary Helen climbed into his white Cadillac and pulled away from the house. The big sign in the rear window that read, "Just Married" was a bit premature, but they'd likely get there, sometime.

Mile-High Addiction

by *William D. Hicks*

The space was tiny
In the airplane lavatory.
Flying 35,000 feet
Above ground
Didn't stop me
From having my way
With two flight attendants.
Count them
Two.
And it was
Only a two-hour flight.
She was lovely
With silken blonde hair.
He was handsome
With a mane
of chest curls.
Different people
In so many ways.
Liking similar things.

A nibble on the neck.
A nibble on the nip.
A peck on the cheek.
A peck on the ear.
Neither knew
I'd been with the other.
And would be
With many others
That very same day.
Oblivious
They were both
To my need
To satisfy
The urge
Some called
Lust
Others called
Addiction.

Biographies for the John

Gail Cohen has been writing anything that pays money (and many things that don't) for nearly 50 years. She has authored or contributed to a dozen books, had her work published in consumer newspapers and magazines and drafted enough promotional copy (on paper) to get Al Gore's dander up. Cohen's *George's Wictionary!* a fictional homage to George Bush's dubious language skills, was published by AuthorHouse in 2008. She has taught writing at Chicago-area universities and hopes she hasn't lead too many writing students astray with her unbridled optimism for a profession that requires food stamps and tenacity more than talent.

Jennifer Djordjevic is a graduate of National Louis University, having earned her bachelor's degree in Psychology and her Master's degree in Written Communication. She spearheaded the University's first literary anthology, *Mosaic,* and has written for local publications including *Quintessential Barrington, For Her Information and Today's Chicago Woman.* Besides spending most of her time working, Jennifer relishes the time she spends with her husband, family, friends and three very hairy cats: Cleo, Meow and Sophie. Writing a book about bathrooms has been fun, but Jen's ready to "wash her hands" of the subject.

William D. Hicks is a writer who lives in Illinois by himself (any offers?). Contrary to popular belief, he is not related to the famous comedian Bill Hicks, though he can be just as funny in his own right. If you should meet William and he tries to convince you he REALLY is the famous DEAD comedian Bill Hicks by introducing himself: "Hi, I'm Bill Hicks," just walk away uninterestedly and he'll likely move onto his next "fan." Hicks may someday publish his memoirs, but more likely the finished product will be about the famous comedian Bill Hicks' life.

Barbara Moriarty earned a bachelor's degree in Marketing from DePaul University and a Master's degree in Written Communications from National Louis University. She began her career as a copywriter at Marshall Field's. Her work has appeared in *Mosaic*, a literary anthology of NLU. Barbara works as an advertising manager in Chicago by day and a writer by candlelight. This is her first, but by no means last, attempt at contributing to a larger body of work. Don't count on the next one having anything to do with rest rooms or bathroom behaviors. She's had her "fill" of toilet-related stories.

Tracy Ruppman is delighted to have her piece "Privvy to Private Conversations" included in this book and would like to thank her "*Last Stall*" friends for their support. Tracy has been writing short stories and poetry for most of her life. In 2006 she completed a screenplay adaptation titled "Prairie Avenue" and earned a second master's degree in written communication from National-Louis University. She is currently a Librarian at Loyola University Chicago and lives on the North Side. Tracy can often be found walking along the lakefront, watching a Cubs game, or immersed in the virtual world of Second Life.

Jim Szczepaniak's favorite spot in his home is the rumpus room so he lobbied to make "rumpus room" this book's subject. Greeted by the Suburban Write People with blank stares, the group chose bathrooms instead. Jim's work history includes newspaper reporting and toiling for a major corporation (Never again, he says). His current gig, working for a suburban high school district, allows him to help a diverse group of young people "learn how to learn." Wife Jane has a maiden name that is more dauntingly Polish than Szczepaniak. Jim spends many pleasant moments reading in the bathroom so he appreciates the chance to "give back" by contributing some of his most heartfelt material.

Barbara K. Yohnka's Christmas Eve birth was celebrated by firefighters called to quell sparks coming from the family chimney. More sparks flew when her parochial school teachers tried (unsuccessfully) to exorcise her storytelling devils. An undergraduate degree in education launched Yohnka's career as a high school world literature, language and composition teacher. After earning a master's degree in Written Communications from National-Louis University, Yohnka edited and contributed to the school's publication, *Mosaic*. Her work has appeared in subsequent issues as well as in *Chicago Pride Magazine*. Fulfillment, Yohnka's first novel, was published in 2007. She is shopping her second book, *Legacy*, while completing her third, *Anniversary*.